Also by

Shannon Esposito

The Pet Psychic Mystery Series
KARMA'S A BITCH
LADY LUCK RUNS OUT
SILENCE IS GOLDEN
FOR PETE'S SAKE

The Paws and Pose Mystery Series
FAUX PAS
HIGH JINX
DOG GONE

Pushing Up Daisies

(A Pet Psychic Mystery No.5)

A NOVEL

Shannon Esposito

misterio press

Pushing Up Daisies
(A Pet Psychic Mystery No.5)

Copyright © Shannon Esposito, 2019
Published by misterio press

Visit Shannon Esposito's official website at

www.murderinparadise.com

Printed in The United States of America

* * * * *

Cover by Dar Albert

Formatting by Debora Lewis
deboraklewis@yahoo.com

* * * * *

ISBN-13: 978-1-947287-10-5

For Atlas, forever in our hearts.

CHAPTER ONE

Ruth Russo stepped out of the St. Pete Journal building with an uncharacteristic smile on her face. The box cradled in her arms contained the last contents of her desk—hand sanitizer, Tums, letters and files, her favorite blonde wig. It was the first time she'd set foot outside the building without a disguise, and she felt free at last. Her body was lighter, her mind unburdened. She didn't even mind the slight, leftover drizzle from a summer storm soaking through her blouse as she crossed the dark, deserted parking lot to her car.

This night marked the end of a chapter in her life, but also the beginning of a new one. She'd never imagined herself on TV. Didn't have the face for it, if she was being honest with herself. Or the body, thanks to a successful career as a food critic. But what she did have was tenacity and the willingness to expose local restaurants' claims of farm fresh, wild caught, locally grown and all the other BS they feed unsuspecting customers with a side of wilted greens. Which is exactly what she'd done in an explosive article series that had caught the attention of a TV producer. *A TV producer!* That still sent a zing of excitement right up her spine.

She wasn't quite sure what to expect from signing that contract for a twelve-show series to continue exposing restaurant claims in the new venue. But the world truly was her oyster right now, and she was finally getting her chance to pluck out that pearl.

As she neared her silver Cadillac, A prickling of unease teased the back of her neck. The smell hit her first. It filled her nostrils, clogged her throat and made her gag.

"What the...?" Dropping the box on the blacktop, she covered her nose with both hands and moved slowly toward her car. The clouds parted, and in the sudden moonlight, a pile of glass glittered on the ground next to her car. Her gaze darted to the driver's side window, which had been smashed out.

She gingerly stepped one foot onto the glass to peer into her car. It crunched under her leather loafer. Leaning over, she gasped. Slick, silvery bodies and round, cloudy eyes greeted her.

Someone had filled her car with dead, rotting fish.

"Who would do this?" she whispered.

Only the slight rustle of wind through the palm trees lining the back of the lot answered her.

Anger bubbled up within her, along with bile from the stench. Keeping her nose covered with one hand, she reached in and plucked a note off her dashboard. Tilting it into the moonlight she read:

Your gonna sleep with the fishes traitor!

She blinked back the tears now blurring her vision. Her heart pounding, she glanced around the parking lot. She was so tired of the threats. So tired of being the bad guy. Didn't they understand she just cared about the food industry? She was the reason restaurants tried so hard to please their customers.

Removing her hand from her face she yelled, "It's you're! Y-O-U-apostrophe-R-E you illiterate coward!"

Her voice echoed in the silence and died. With a sniffle, she scooped up the box and marched back into the building to call the police... again.

CHAPTER TWO

For the second day in a row, our morning began with the scent of fried food and thumping music coming from the St. Pete Seafood Festival across the street in Straub Park. Yesterday it had been a real distraction for me and my sister, Mallory, as we'd worked at Darwin's Pet Boutique.

Mallory was helping me out while my business partner and groomer extraordinaire, Sylvia, trekked around Europe on her two-week honeymoon.

But Sundays the pet boutique was closed, so we were finally free to partake in the festivities.

Willow, our middle sister, had volunteered to stay with Grandma Winters—who'd shown up unexpectedly a few days ago—and give her a tour of the less crowded parts of St. Pete. Neither of them was a big fan of crowds or seafood.

Mallory and I stepped out of the townhouse gate in flip-flops and sunhats, both of us grinning like a possum eatin' a sweet potato. Mallory was also holding our current foster puppy, a Yorkie named Petey. We were supposed to be trying to find him a home, but Mallory has gotten real attached to the little guy, so she's been procrastinating.

"Ready?" I asked.

"Born ready." Grabbing my hand with her free one, Mallory pulled me through the stand-still traffic on Beach Drive toward Straub Park.

"Mal, this is jaywalking!" I protested. "Sorry, sorry." I waved to the cars we were weaving our way past.

We were across the street and heading toward the front entrance before she answered me. "Some rules are begging to be broken, Sis." Tugging me faster down the sidewalk, she added, "There's the gate. Is Will meeting you here?"

I smirked and narrowed my eyes at her, as we got in line to buy our tickets. "Yeah, why? Eager to get rid of me?"

"'Course not." But the mischievous gleam in her green eyes said differently.

We'd all grown up in Savannah, Georgia, sheltered from the world by an over-protective mother. I knew Mal was itching to explore the festival alone, to feel independent. Plus, she was boy-crazy, and I'd inherited our mother's overprotective gene.

My stomach gurgled at the mixture of aromas. I eyed the red-and-white-striped awnings of the vendor booths scattered around the park beneath a cloudless, azure sky. Good heavens there was an overwhelming array of foods available. How would we ever choose?

Mallory pushed me through the crowd and steered me toward a booth. *Well, that answers that question.* "I know you're having lunch with Will, but we can grab something small."

I glanced up at the sign as we waited in line. "Tempura fried ice cream?"

"Yes, dessert first, my treat. Live a little." She pulled cash out of her jean shorts pocket. When it was our turn, she said, "Two, please."

I held up my hand. "Just one." I didn't have anything on my stomach except a cup of tea. At eighteen, Mallory could still get away with eating sugar for breakfast without feeling sick as a dog. I couldn't.

Mallory's hand went to her hip as she glanced at me. "Prude."

"I'll have a bite of yours," I said in the spirit of compromise.

"Here, hold Petey." She transferred the weightless ball of fluff to me. While he struggled to nibble my chin with his sharp puppy teeth, Mallory accepted the Styrofoam bowl. In it sat a fried, golden globe, which was cut in half to showcase the green ice cream, then drizzled with chocolate syrup. "Now this here is real magic." She grinned.

Taking a bite as we walked away, she moaned. "Heaven." Then she threaded her arm through mine. "Come on, let's go watch the band while you help me eat this."

We took a seat at the end of a long banquet table. I checked the ground by my feet for red ant piles, and finding none, I sat Petey down in the shade beneath the table.

He licked my toe and then stretched out and yipped at a grasshopper in his high puppy voice.

"Oh, my stars!" Mallory said, pointing her spoon at the five musicians playing their hearts out on the raised stage. "That's Brad Rose! The one with the red guitar. I heard he was leaving The Firestarters.

This must be his new band. I can't believe he's here!"

I eyed the object of my sister's admiration. "Kinda has a Keith Urban vibe going on."

"Yeah, except way younger... and hotter." She pushed the ice cream toward me without taking her eyes off the young man with the red guitar.

Oh boy. I rolled my eyes. *Target acquired.*

I put a little dab of ice cream on the spoon and offered it to Petey. His tiny tongue lapped it up, and then he sneezed and rolled over on his back. Slipping off a flip-flop, I rubbed his soft belly with my toe.

My phone buzzed in my pocket. It was Will. *Thank heavens.* I wasn't sure how long I could sit here and watch my sister drool. "Hey, Mal, that's Will. I'm going to go meet him at the front gate. You want to keep Petey with you?"

"Yeah, sure." She held out her hand, her attention still riveted to the stage.

Sighing, I placed the end of the leash in her hand. "Text me when you're done watching the band, and I'll let you know where we are."

I found Will waiting just inside the entrance. Even dressed in old workout clothes and a worn-thin baseball cap, he still made my heart flutter. "Hey, you." I smiled as I removed my sunhat and slipped into his arms. He was damp with sweat, but I didn't care.

"Sorry, snuck a run in before I came."

He tried to pull away, but I held him tight. "If you think I'm going to let you go because of a little sweat, you don't know me very well, Detective."

I'd meant it as a joke, but a wave of Will's insecurity washed over me. *Shoot.* I knew my friendship with Zach Faraday—half-human, half-jinn and all male—was probably the cause of that. And from the shocking news Grandma Winters had brought us about Father, I knew things were about to get harder for Will in that department.

Nothing I could do about it right now, though. Leaning back a bit, I looked up into his eyes, which matched the color of the sky today. "Hungry?"

"Starving." From the way his eyes swept over my face and landed on my mouth, I suddenly got the idea he wasn't talking about food.

I grinned and plopped my sunhat back on. "Me too. Come on."

He took my hand in his as we navigated the crowd. "Where's Mallory? Thought she was coming with you."

I stopped short as two squealing boys running with ice cream bowls almost plowed into me. "Sorry!" A harried lady running after them said as she passed.

"No harm done," I called after her. We continued walking. "Yeah, Mal's here. I left her droolin' all over some guy in the country-pop band that's playing right now."

Will chuckled and listened to the music for a second. "Well, at least he's not just a pretty face, sounds talented." And then he stopped dead in his tracks in the middle of the crowd.

I glanced up at his expression. It was frozen, his eyes crinkled in the corners under the shade of his ball cap. His body tensed up beside me. His grip on my hand tightened.

"Will?" He didn't answer. I followed his gaze and saw her.

Cynthia. Will's ex-wife.

I'd seen pictures of her one night when we were going through his photo albums. She was even more stunning in person with long, silky hair, a curvy figure, and a confident strut. The complete opposite of me, with my lanky frame and short, frost-white hair. After five years of marriage she'd left Will for a German plastic surgeon. That was almost seven years ago.

She spotted Will at the same time and made her way toward him. Her smile widened until it lit up her whole face.

"Will! I was hoping I'd run into you here." Her eyes swept over me dismissively and then locked back on Will, who still hadn't moved. Her smile faltered but her chest puffed out. "Happy to see me?"

Will finally cleared his throat. "What brings you back to the states?"

We both glanced down at her hand at the same time. No wedding band.

Crap on a cracker.

"I've moved back to St. Pete actually." She shifted her ample hip and tilted her head. I could see her trying to figure out if that pleased Will.

Double crap.

Will's body was stiff, his arms crossed. "Didn't work out with Hans, huh?"

Her mouth curved a little but fell short of a smile. Her eyes, the color of sunlit honey, filled with regret. "You could say that. Anyway, I was really homesick, so here I am. Home."

Silence stretched out between them as Will refused to take the bait. "How's Toffee?" he asked, changing the subject. Toffee was their cat, which she'd taken with her when she'd left.

Cynthia's chin dipped, but she watched Will carefully from beneath lush, dark lashes. "Still alive, though he's pretty much deaf and just likes to lounge around. No more chasing lizards." She lifted her head and a dimple punctuated her smile. "You should come by and see him. I've bought a place over on 11th Avenue. I'm going to restore it."

Suddenly she gasped and jumped back a step. Water had sloshed out of the cup she was holding and soaked the front of her white, silk shirt. "What in the world?"

My face burned. *Oops.* I really needed to get control of my water magick during emotional upsets. Though, who in the world wears silk to a seafood festival?

A woman dressing to impress her ex, that's who.

Will took the distraction as an opportunity to cut the conversation short. Grabbing my hand, he said, "Darwin and I are meeting someone, so we have to go. See you around."

I watched her open her mouth to protest, but she was too flustered to get anything out before Will pulled me past her, and we disappeared into the crowd.

I snuck a glance up at him. His nostrils were flared, jaw set tight.

"Well," I said, "that was awkward."

Will took a breath and slowed down. "Yeah, sorry I didn't introduce you. It was just a shock to see her in town again."

"It's okay." But was it? She obviously had her sights set on him again. I needed to get his mind off of her quickly. "Hey, there's a booth from that sushi place Frankie's been raving about. Come on."

I led him over to the booth with the Happi Sushi banner stretched above the spread of food, and we got in line behind a dozen other hungry festivalgoers.

When it was finally our turn, the young man in a backwards ball cap and white apron smiled at us. "What can I get for you folks?"

I eyed the silver trays nestled in ice and decorated with lettuce and dozens of colorful displays of sushi pieces. They were like works of art.

"What do you recommend? Everything looks good," Will said, reading my mind.

As he and the aproned man talked, I couldn't help but notice the argument going on in the background. A young Japanese woman, her dark hair pulled up in a knot on top her head, gripped a gold lobster statue in her fist and was shaking it at a large, well-built Black man with shoulder-length dreadlocks. His hands rested lightly on his hips, and his head was bowed.

Will followed my gaze. "Oh...whoa... that's Ogden Stewart."

I glanced up at the star-struck expression on his face. "Who?"

"Ogden Stewart. Best Tampa Bay defensive end and linebacker we've ever had. Holds the fifth all-time career sacks record, all-time leader in fumble return touchdowns and was the NFL Defensive Player of the Year in 2010."

The aproned man glanced back at Ogden and then nodded. "These days Oggie's retired. He's a nice guy and Hana's boyfriend. She owns Happi Sushi. You wanna meet him?"

We were all staring as Hana tossed the gold lobster statue into a large plastic trash can behind her and crossed her arms.

Oggie lifted his hands in a 'what did you do that for?' gesture.

"Maybe now's not the best time," Will said. "Why'd he retire? He's only in his thirties, right?"

"Yeah. He was forced out when they discovered he has post-concussion syndrome."

"Rough game." Will shook his head. "Too bad. All right. You've sold me on the barbequed eel sashimi and the volcano roll. We'll take two orders of each. Darwin, want to add anything? California rolls?"

"Sure," I said, suddenly distracted by a snuffling on my toe. I glanced down. A miniature dachshund was poking its head out from beneath the white tablecloth.

"Well, hello there," I said, bending down.

The dog belly-crawled out further and sniffed the air. Expressive, brown eyes peered up at my face. It had a black and tan, smooth coat, and looked pretty young. When my hand got too close, it let out a warning bark.

"All right." I held my hand where it was. "You come to me."

"That's Daisy," the man behind the table said, peering over. "Hana's dog. She talks tough but she's harmless. The dog, not Hana." He snorted at some private joke.

"Well, hello there, Daisy girl," I cooed.

She pushed herself up on short, stocky legs and touched her cold nose to my hand.

Zap!

I jerked my hand away as energy zipped through me, carrying a vision: The heavy smell of spicy cologne, a male voice and female voice arguing, a man's huge black sneakers, a glass bowl shattering against the wall, a wave of panic.

Standing abruptly, I held my sunhat on while I jogged in place. The familiar pop of energy leaving my body came after a few seconds. It was a small energy discharge, so the argument must not have been too traumatic for Daisy.

Glancing over at Hana, I felt a ping of empathy. Didn't seem like she and Oggie were doing too good in the relationship department.

Will caught my eye as I stopped jogging. He smirked and looked down at Daisy, who'd scooted back under the tablecloth, startled by my sudden movement. Just her curious, liquid black eyes and long nose peered out at us.

Well, that was an improvement in Will's reaction.

Is he getting comfortable with me receiving psychic visions from traumatized animals?

Encouraged, I knelt and coaxed Daisy back out. "Sorry, girl. Didn't mean to startle you." I softly scratched beneath her long, floppy ears. Her tongue reached out and licked my arm. "Aren't you a sweetheart. Better get back in the shade, though. It's hot as hades out here today." I lifted up the tablecloth. She gifted me a panting grin then disappeared.

When I stood, I saw Hana fall into Ogden's arms. Tears ran in shiny streaks down her face. Ogden kissed the top of her head. I quickly turned away, giving them their moment of privacy. Relationships sure weren't easy.

Will and I made our way back toward the band, the bag of sushi dangling from Will's hand. "So," he said, "what happened with the dog?"

I glanced up at him. His eyes met mine, and I saw curiosity, not fear or judgment. Dare I say *acceptance*? Was he trying harder because he felt he was competing with Zach? Either way, he was definitely trying.

"I saw an argument between a man and woman. I'm assuming the dog's owner, Hana, and her boyfriend. I couldn't see faces, just some big male sneakers, and couldn't make out words, just the tone. A glass bowl was thrown against the wall. Scared Daisy a bit, but she wasn't hurt."

"It's kind of like psychic eavesdropping, isn't it?" Will teased. Then he slipped an arm around my shoulder. "Guess that could come in handy."

My heart expanded, and the sun seemed brighter. If he was getting comfortable with my visions, maybe I should take another shot at explaining my elemental magick to him? The last time I'd tried had been such a disaster, but I really needed him to know and accept all of me. Otherwise, what's the point of us being together?

CHAPTER THREE

By the time we reached the table where I'd left Mal, the band was on a break and the stage was empty.

"Where'd my sister disappear to now?" I sighed, scanning the crowd. "She was supposed to text me when they were done."

Will pointed to the right side of the stage, under an oak tree. "There she is."

My eyes narrowed as I realized who she was sitting on the grass with. *Of course.* "Come on."

"Hey there, Mal," I said, eyeing Brad Rose. His glossy black hair was swept over one eye, and his red guitar leaned against the tree beside him. "Hi, I'm Darwin, Mallory's sister."

He nodded, not bothering to stand up. "How's it going?"

Folding my arms, I pointed my chin toward Will. "And this here is Detective Will Blake. Homicide unit."

Mallory scooped Petey up and pushed herself off the ground. She shot me a look that held a different kind of fire. Her face was flushed, which didn't happen from the Florida heat, she was immune to that. It only came from the type of heat an attractive male caused.

Brad Rose sketched a salute at Will. His bottom lip piercing glinted in the sunlight as he smirked. "What's up?"

Will silently gave him the once over.

I forced the irritation from my tone as I said, "Mal, we're going to sit down and eat. We have extra. Join us?"

"Not hungry." Her brows rose over glittering eyes. A warning for me to back off. Then she placed Petey in my arms. "Take him with you, will ya? Brad's going to let me play his guitar before they go back on."

"How nice of Brad." I'm sure she caught my sugary, sarcastic tone, but she ignored it. I was also sure she didn't give a lick what I thought right now. I smoothed Petey's hair back from his eyes. "Fine." Before I left, I glared at Brad. "Don't give her any alcohol, she's only eighteen."

"You're turning into Mom," Mallory threw at my back.

As Will unpacked the sushi, I pulled a collapsible silicone dog bowl—one of our best-selling summer items—from my straw bag and filled it with fresh water. Petey lapped up a few mouthfuls, then stuck a paw in the bowl and started digging.

I shook my head and laughed. "You're a trip." I looked up at Will with a groan. "I'm getting too attached to this little guy, too. I've got to find him a home before Mallory talks me into keeping him."

Will slipped a pair of wooden chopsticks from their wrapping. "It shouldn't be hard to find a home for a purebred puppy, should it?"

I picked up the other pair of chopsticks. "It is when you don't actually tell anyone the puppy needs a home."

As we ate, I kept an eye on Mallory. She'd removed her sunhat. Her long, auburn hair was draped over one shoulder, and she alternated between stroking Brad's guitar, and looking adoringly into his eyes. He slid behind her and put his hand on top of hers.

I think I growled out loud.

Will followed my gaze. "Want me to do a background check on him?"

"Can you do that?" I asked, completely serious.

The corner of Will's mouth twitched with amusement. "She's technically an adult and a smart girl. I'm sure she'll be fine."

I popped a piece of California roll in my mouth and sulked while I chewed. "She's only dated one guy before, and you remember how that turned out. She's naïve."

Will reached across the table and squeezed my hand. "And the cure for that is experience."

I sighed. He was right. I'd been naïve when I'd first moved to St. Pete, too. But I'd gotten lucky right out of the gate by meeting Will. I watched him struggle to open a packet of soy sauce with his teeth. A swell of gratitude rolled over me. I really was lucky. Sometimes it was easy to take him for granted. I shouldn't do that.

"Thanks for..." I felt myself choke up. I didn't even know what I wanted to say. "For being you."

His eyes sparkled playfully as they met mine. Tossing the packet on the table, he pressed his warm lips against my knuckles then grinned. "You're welcome."

"Ladies and gentlemen, we're only minutes away from the start of the Chef's Showdown, where eleven chefs from local restaurants will go head to head in five different seafood categories, competing to win the coveted Golden Lobster Award. Four judges will cast their votes, and the winner will be announced this evening at 5:00 pm. So, come on over to the Chef's Tent Exhibition to watch the judging and cheer on your local favorite."

I removed my sunhat and fanned myself with it. "Golden Lobster Award? Wonder if it's an actual golden lobster like the one Hana from Happi Sushi threw in the trash?"

"Don't know." Will packed up the empty containers and shoved them back in the bag. "Want to take a walk over there and check it out? I'll probably be hungry again in five minutes anyway."

"Are you just trying to keep me from ruining Mal's chance at a date with Mr. Rock Star?"

"Yes." Will scooped up the bag and flashed me a grin that I'd follow anywhere. "Come on, Ms. Overprotective."

We stopped at a wine tasting table on the way there, so I ended up with a plastic cup of Riesling in one hand and Petey in the other. I wasn't trying to baby the Yorkie—which I was constantly chiding Mallory for—I just didn't want him to get stepped on. This was a big crowd, lots of opportunity to get trampled.

We were standing off to the side, sipping our wine and waiting for the judges to taste the first round of appetizers when I spotted my friend, Frankie, in the crowd. "Will, can you get Frankie's attention?" I asked, since I didn't have any free hands.

Will stuck two fingers in his mouth and let out a sharp whistle. When Frankie turned, he waved her over.

"Hey, y'all!" Her hug was scented with sunscreen and mango body lotion. "You remember Minnie, right?"

"Sure! Hey, Minnie." I shook her hand. I'd met her before at Pirate City—a stretch of makeshift shelters in the woods where the homeless lived. She looked different. Happier and cleaned up with a new, shoulder-length haircut and a crisp, yellow sundress.

I'm sure Frankie'd had something to do with that. She used to be one of the homeless, too, until she'd won millions in the Florida lottery a few years back. She's never forgotten where she came from, though.

"And this is Spider." Frankie motioned to the guy standing behind her. His eyes were cast down and while his hair was combed, it was greasy, and sweat had left a dark streak down the side of his dusty cheek. That and his scruffy clothes suggested he was homeless.

"Nice to meet you." Spider didn't look Will in the eye when he shook his hand, though he smiled at me before ducking his head.

"Hello, Petey darling!" Frankie scratched under the Yorkie's chin, and he began to squirm in my arms. "Here, let me take him for a minute. Give you a break."

I let her slide Petey from my arm and then asked, "Where's your girls?" Her two Chihuahuas usually went everywhere with her.

She rolled her eyes. "At home. Itty ate one of my house plants, which thank the good Lord in heaven wasn't toxic, but she's thrown up a few times. The vet said to just give her access to plenty of water and let her rest. I didn't want to leave her alone, so Bitty stayed, too." She laughed as Petey nipped at her chin. "Aren't you feisty today." As she stroked the top of his head, chunky gold bracelets slid down her freckled arm and caught Petey's attention. He tried to attack them but couldn't reach.

"Hope she feels better soon. If not, let me know, I've got some flower essence that might—"

"Okay folks," the announcer interrupted over crackling speakers. "Our Chef's Showdown has begun. For round one, the judges have appetizers in front of them, which had to be created from the ingredients given to the chefs. Good luck, everyone!"

Frankie leaned in. With a conspiratorial tone, she said, "You know who the judge on the end is? The woman with short, dark hair?"

We all glanced at the dark-haired woman, watching as she snapped a photo of the dish in front of her with her cell phone, before digging her fork in.

"No, who is she?" I asked.

"That's none other than Ruth "the Ruthless" Russo, the infamous food critic. Nobody knew what she looked like until now. Today is her public debut."

"Really?" I watched Ruth Russo pick up a pen and write something. "Isn't going out in public to restaurants sort of a job requirement? How'd no one know what she looked like before now?"

Frankie moved Petey to rest in her other arm. "They do go out in public, but she always wore disguises. Wigs and stuff. She's not very well-liked in the restaurant world, to say the least. Loathed is more like it. She's given some scathing reviews over the years. Been responsible for the failures of dozens of restaurants."

I eyed Ruth Russo. Must feel good to finally be out in public without a disguise. Or not. If she was that hated, she might still be worried about folks knowing who she really is. "I understand why she'd want to stay anonymous. But why's she showing her face now?"

"Apparently she just retired from the newspaper business and has been hired to do a TV show. One of those shows that exposes how restaurants misrepresent and sometimes flat out lie to their customers about where their food comes from."

"Can't imagine that's going to improve her reputation," Will said.

"I don't think she cares at this point." Frankie dug some cash out of her bright orange, linen short's pocket and handed it to Spider. "Be a doll and get us all some of those crab cakes, will ya?"

"Yes, ma'am." He was still staring at the hundred-dollar bill in his hand as he walked away.

"You think he's coming back?" Minnie looked concerned as she reached over and scratched under Petey's chin. His eyes squinted in pleasure as he ate up the attention.

"Have faith, darlin'." Frankie winked at her, then leaned toward me. "Spider's a recovering opioid and heroin addict. Just got out of his third stay at rehab. Poor guy has some permanent brain damage from an overdose back in March."

My heart squeezed as I watched him navigate through the crowd. "He's got a long road ahead of him. By the nickname I assume he's living at Pirate City?" No one used their real name there. Mac, a long-time resident of the homeless camp, seemed to be in charge of giving everyone nicknames. At least he'd given me mine, Snow White.

"Yeah." She wiped at the sweat rolling down her temple. "First night there, he ended up sleeping on top of the picnic table instead of in his tent when a wolf spider tried to make friends." She chuckled to herself. "Anyway, Mac's lookin' out for him." She turned her attention to Minnie. "Our girl here is out though. Got a cute little trailer over on 4th Street and a full-time job cleanin' rooms at the Comfort Inn."

"Congrats, Minnie, that's great news." I was glad she wasn't living in the homeless camp anymore. It was dangerous enough to live there as a male. Being female, I'm sure meant she had a very different kind of danger to worry about.

As Frankie was catching us up on all the local gossip, Spider returned. He'd been gone awhile, but Frankie and Minnie shared a relieved smile when he held out a wad of money. Pocketing it, Frankie squeezed his shoulder. "Proud of you."

Spider's face looked stricken for a moment, but then he dropped his head and held up the plate of crab cakes.

"Looks delicious," Frankie said, taking one.

My attention moved from Spider to Frankie. She hadn't seemed to notice his odd reaction to her praise.

I pushed the thought aside as a few of my regular customers from the pet boutique stopped by to chat and watch the contest with us.

By the time the judges were on their last course, I was getting nervous about leaving Mallory alone for so long. I opened my mouth to tell Will we should head back to find her when there was a sudden commotion at the judges table.

Ruth Russo popped out of her chair and fell forward, knocking over the folding table and sending all the contents spilling into the grass. There was a collective gasp from the crowd. Pushing herself off the toppled table, she whirled around and started throwing up in the trash can behind her. The other three judges jumped up from their chairs. They huddled together, glancing nervously at each other as the surrounding crowd grew silent.

Will threaded himself through the bystanders toward the commotion. I followed closely behind. Ruth Russo was still vomiting when we reached her.

"Ma'am, are you okay?" Will asked.

She leaned both hands on the edge of the trash can. Her skin glistened with sweat and she was panting hard. Lifting a shaking hand, she tugged on the neckline of her shirt. "I... I can't breathe."

Will pulled out his phone and dialed 911. "Any paramedics here?" he shouted.

Two women pushed through the crowd. "We're nurses." They hurried over and helped Ruth back into her chair. One of them grabbed a water bottle, the other checked Ruth's pulse with two fingers on her wrist. Ruth's breathing was even more labored, her dark eyes wild with fear.

The nurse checking her pulse glanced back at Will. She stared at him meaningfully. "Tell them to hurry."

Four minutes rolled by like molasses in the winter. We all watched helplessly as Ruth Russo gasped for breath.

I held my hand protectively to my own throat as her panic washed over me.

Two paramedics finally pushed through the crowd carrying a gurney. As they tended to Ruth, Will called the nurses over.

"That doesn't look like heat exhaustion." His voice was heavy with concern.

They shared a glance. The taller brunette shook her head. "Honestly, with the vomiting, the low blood pressure, arrhythmia and the fact that her lips and tongue are numb... I wouldn't rule out poisoning."

After a moment of stunned silence, Will glanced over at Ruth Russo being carried away on the gurney. He pulled out his phone.

CHAPTER FOUR

It didn't take long for St. Pete PD to arrive, with the crime scene investigators right behind them. They got busy taping off a large area that encompassed both the table and the spilled contents strewn in the grass.

Will motioned to two officers. When they approached, he said, "I just spoke to the health department. They want the festival shut down until we can say for sure if Russo was poisoned or not and what exactly she ate. Find the festival coordinator and make the announcement. Clear everyone out."

A crime scene investigator wearing protective gloves and booties began slowly circling and videotaping the area, while a second investigator in protective gear approached Will. "What exactly are we thinking here?"

Will had his hands on his hips, his gaze sweeping over the scene. "Possible poisoning, but not sure what the source is. Unfortunately, the victim knocked over the table, so we can't be sure which of the items in the grass were in front of her. Just collect as many samples as you can. Plastic cups included. I'll see if the other judges can help us out with what she consumed."

I waited until the investigator walked away and touched his arm. "I'm gonna go find Mal, so we can get out of your way."

"Okay." He squeezed my hand. "I'll call you later."

I nodded, but my insides twisted. I wasn't sure I'd be free to take his call, and he definitely wouldn't like the reason why.

I let Frankie know the festival would be shutting down and then made my way back through the crowd, cradling Petey close to my chest.

A man wearing a red baseball cap caught my attention. He stood out to me because his expression wasn't one of concern as he watched the police work. In fact, there was a subtle smile on his face.

I pulled my phone out with my free hand and snapped a photo of him. The speakers crackled, and then the announcement came that the seafood festival would be closing. Time to find Mal and skedaddle.

-✻- -✻- -✻-

When Mal and I got back home, the townhouse was empty. Willow and Grandma Winters weren't back yet. Good, it'd give me a chance to take Goldie, my golden retriever, for a walk and then get ready for the unpleasant night ahead. "Hey, girl."

Goldie greeted us by turning in happy circles and whining, her tail swishing back and forth.

I stroked her head and then sat Petey down so Goldie could give him her usual once-over. Petey was evidently tired from his big adventure. He only gave her one little sniff and then flopped on his side in his doggie bed beside the sofa.

Mallory lifted her black cat, Lucky, from the counter and cradled her in her arms. As she snuggled her nose in Lucky's fur, the cat purred loudly and rubbed her cheek against Mallory's. "Well, that makes two of us who are happy," Mallory said, grinning.

Brad Rose had asked her out. There would be no living with her now.

I rolled my eyes. "You know he's going to be off to some other city in a week. I wouldn't get too attached."

"It's just a date. I'm not planning on marrying the guy." Mallory sprawled out on the sofa with Lucky stretched out on her chest.

"Good to know. You should be concentrating on your graphic design program anyway. How are classes going?" I grabbed Goldie's leash and snapped it on her collar, getting a lick on the wrist.

"Just fine, thank you very much... Mom."

"You should be happy you have a sister who cares so much," I threw over my shoulder, as I stepped into the elevator with Goldie.

My stomach clenched as my thoughts turned to this evening. Zach was back in town and would be our dinner guest, by Grandma Winter's request. I hadn't seen Zach since our "moment" at Sylvia's wedding six days ago. And I had no idea what Grandma Winters had up her sleeve. It had something to do with helping our father, but that's all I knew.

❧ ❧ ❧

I was pouring water into the glasses on the dining room table when Zach arrived. Everyone else was in the kitchen.

Willow pulled rolls from the oven. The scent of warm bread wafted through the house.

Goldie and Petey greeted Zach with wagging tails when the elevator door opened. Lucky stayed on her perch on the back of the sofa, ears back, eyes glowing, her tail flicking in irritation. She wasn't Zach's biggest fan, even though her original owner had been Zach's mother. I wondered if Lucky could sense his jinn nature.

He was wearing his signature black jeans and black t-shirt pulled taut against his thick chest and arms. His dark hair was spiked up in the front. I thought about the intricate black tribal tattoo that I knew graced his chest. The one that had glowed under my touch when he'd invaded my dreams. My jaw clenched as I forced the thought away. I watched him greet the dogs and then straighten up, letting his dark, glittering eyes find mine. "Darwin."

My name in his mouth never failed to raise the hair on my arms. A familiar heat washed over me. I steeled myself against it and cleared my throat. "Thanks for coming tonight."

He stepped forward and handed me a bottle of wine. "My pleasure." Our fingertips touched as I accepted it, sending a jolt of energy through my body. By the way his eyes hooded over, I knew he'd felt it, too. He took a deep breath in and then pulled his gaze away from mine with obvious effort to greet the rest of my family.

They were all staring at him from the kitchen. My sisters' expressions held a mix of fear and curiosity. But Grandma Winters's eyes were two hard emerald stones glinting with suspicion. She'd warned me jinn were dangerous, so it wasn't a shock, just a reminder that this dinner was going to be uncomfortable.

Grandma Winters stepped forward and introduced herself to Zach. I'd never seen her interact with anyone but our family, so it was strange viewing her through an outsider's eyes. She was a slight woman, only five-two, and her heart-shaped face was framed by a silvery pixie-cut. She wore one of her signature outfits: a long-sleeved, purple, flower-patterned blouse and white cotton bell slacks. Her powdery soft skin sported a few deep crow's feet at the corners of her eyes. Despite not taking up a lot of physical space, she radiated a strong energy that you could feel up close. I wondered if Zach felt it now.

"Nice to finally meet you," Zach said, though his posture was uncharacteristically stiff and tense.

Yeah, he felt it.

Zach moved away from her, leaning on the kitchen bar. "Mallory, Willow... good to see you two again. I didn't realize you were still in St. Pete."

When I saw neither of them were going to answer him, I stepped in. "I'm trying to talk them into moving here, actually." They weren't comfortable leaving Mom back in Savannah all by herself, but at least I knew they were staying until this whole thing with our father was sorted out.

Willow shot me an undecipherable look as she left the kitchen with the basket of rolls to put on the table. Mallory just stared at Zach with her arms folded. They both took Grandma Winters's warning about jinn as fact and didn't understand my friendship with him. Ignoring their slight, he turned to Grandma Winters. "You're the reason I'm here?"

She gave a half-nod of concession. "Ash Winters is, actually. But yes, I've requested your presence. We need your help."

Zach looked sharply at me, his eyes narrowing. He knew a little about our father. He was the one who'd discovered—and told me—about our father being *Tuath De'*, a race of people from another dimension with the ability to manipulate the elements of nature. It was where my sisters and I had inherited our elemental gifts. Our mother was a mere mortal from North Carolina. Zach didn't look particularly happy about the possibility of being dragged into my father's mess, but he finally nodded. "Well, something smells delicious. Shall we?" He motioned to the table.

"I'll just open this bottle," I said, hurrying into the kitchen. I was sure we were going to need it.

I spent the first twenty minutes of dinner picking at my baked pasta while Grandma Winters grilled Zach on his jinn background, his deceased Gypsy mother, and how much he knew about our father. When she got to the question of how Zach intrudes on my dreams, her posture straightened. She had gotten to the point of why he was here. I dropped my fork and took a large swallow of wine, regretting that I'd confessed that to her.

Zach seemed to sense the significance of her question, also. "This is what you need me for? The dream traveling?"

We were staring at Grandma Winters. She nodded solemnly. "The girls have all made contact with Ash in their dream state. As you know, the dream state is one door into *Sidhe*. This is going to be the key to freeing him. Since Darwin's element is water, she's the one who needs to go, but I don't want her going alone. I'd like you to be there, to protect her."

Zach and I shared a surprised glance. Goldie was stretched out beneath the table, and I ran my bare foot across her back for comfort. Then I asked the obvious question. "So, we're going to attempt a prison break?"

Grandma Winters laced her thin fingers in front of her. The pink diamond on her ring finger caught the light and my eye. I'd always loved that ring. Not just because it was a stunning two carat princess-cut stone, but because her first love had created it for her. She'd let me try it on once on my fifteenth birthday, and I'd noticed how the silver band had worn thin over time. I'd also felt the strong energy signature of their love attached to the ring. I forced my attention back on her words.

"While it's true Ash was imprisoned in *Sidhe* for breaking the rules and having children with a human, he was due to be released last month. Unfortunately, his guardian, a vicious mer-woman named Iris, has decided she doesn't want to be without his company. She's taken him and moved him to an unknown location. He's her prisoner illegally now."

Zach's eyes were suddenly lit with red embers. "Iris. Yes, we're acquainted."

Grandma Winters nodded. I'd already filled her in on Zach protecting me and Goldie from an attack by Iris and her sea-wolf. Probably where she got the idea of Zach going with me for protection. "So, you understand why I can't send Darwin after her father alone. Are you willing to help?"

We were all silent and still, waiting for Zach's answer. He met my gaze and I watched the emotions flicker across his face... anger, fear, frustration, sadness.

"I am bound to protect Darwin, as I'm sure you understand. So, I will do whatever is required to keep her safe and happy." His hand moved forward, like he was going to reach for mine, but he stopped himself. He sat up straighter in his chair and turned back to Grandma Winters, who was watching us both carefully. "I'll see if I can find out anything about where Ash is being held. When do we do this?"

"I have to ready Darwin." Grandma Winters turned to me, a stern gleam in her eye. "You have to get full control of your water magick before we attempt this."

My face warmed. "I—" Just then my cell phone vibrated on the kitchen counter. I jumped up, glad for the distraction. "That's probably Will." Aware of all eyes on me, I answered the phone with my back turned. "Hey, Will."

"Hey, Darwin. Listen, I'm at the hospital."

My heart flipped in my chest. "Still? What's going on?"

The fatigue weighed heavy in his voice. "It's Ruth Russo. She didn't make it."

"Oh my heavens!" I spun around and stared at my family, thinking about the last time I saw the poor woman. "I can't believe it. How?"

"The toxicology reports are still out, but the doctor says it looks like classic Tetrodotoxin poisoning. Poisoning from a pufferfish."

My legs felt wobbly. I lowered myself onto the bar stool. "So, she accidently ate a poisonous fish?"

"Or not so accidently. According to the other judges, she was eating pufferfish when she had the reaction. Remember Frankie telling us she wasn't well liked?" There was some rustling. "Then again, all four of the judges were eating the pufferfish, and Russo was the only one who got sick." A frustrated sigh. "I gotta go. I'll give you a call in the morning."

"You look like somebody died," Mallory said, as I walked slowly back to the table.

An image of Ruth Russo, still very much alive, being carried away on the gurney was stuck in the forefront of my mind.

How can a life be over just like that? One minute she's munching on some seafood and the next, boom. Gone.

"Someone did." I lowered myself back down into the chair. Goldie must've felt my distress as she rested her head on my lap under the table. I slid my fingers into her fur. "That woman at the seafood festival who got sick. The one they closed the seafood festival over. Apparently, she was poisoned... by accident or not. Will doesn't know yet."

❖   ❖   ❖

After Zach left and Grandma Winters had retired for the evening, my sisters and I stayed up talking. I tossed Goldie's stuffed gator across the room, and it landed by the French doors that led out to the patio. She trotted after it with Petey on her heels, trying to bite her tail.

Mallory had her laptop balanced on her thighs and a cup of tea in one hand. She was searching for information on Ruth Russo. "Stop that, Lucky." She blocked the cat's face with her free hand. Lucky gagged. "That's what you get for eating my hair." She shifted so she could pull her hair out of the cat's mouth. Then she set her teacup down and said, "Apparently Ruth Russo had been a restaurant critic for the St. Pete Journal for eighteen years. Recently she signed on for a twelve-show TV series to expose restaurants' false claims of farm fresh and locally sourced ingredients."

Lucky batted Mallory's ponytail with her paw but it didn't break her concentration.

"Here's an interview with Ruth Russo dated two months ago. She says, 'For restaurants' fish claims that seemed well... fishy to me, I snuck out samples by keeping zip-top baggies in my purse. The St. Pete journal then sent them off to the University of Florida to have them DNA tested, to see if they were the type of fish the restaurant claimed they were serving. I can't tell you how many times I've caught a local restaurant claiming its fish and chips were wild Alaskan Pollock, when the DNA test showed it was actually frozen Chinese Pollock treated with the preservative sodium tripolyphosphate." Mallory glanced up at us with a disgusted look on her face. "I can't believe they get away with that. Gross."

Goldie dropped Gator in my lap and stared at me, ears tilted forward, mouth open in a grin. I chucked it across the room again.

Petey scratched at my shin. Apparently, he was done with the game. I lifted him up onto my lap and adjusted the blue striped t-shirt Mallory had him dressed in. Yawning, he curled into a ball and closed his eyes.

"Well, I can definitely see why she'd have enemies in the restaurant business," I said.

"Huh," came from Willow. She was wearing a "There is No Planet B" t-shirt, sitting cross-legged in the chair, her fingers absentmindedly braiding her hair. "You think a restaurant owner poisoned her for exposing their deception?"

I shrugged, stroking Petey's plum-sized, silky head with my thumb. "Seems like a pretty good motive... if she was poisoned on purpose. Will did say she was eating pufferfish when she had the reaction. Mal, can you look up why people eat pufferfish if it's so poisonous?"

We watched as she typed something in. The monitor light added an otherworldly glow to her green eyes. "Here we go. Apparently in Japan, it's an expensive delicacy. They call it fugu and because of the high risk of poisoning their customers, chefs have to go through three years of training to get a license to serve it." Her eyes widened. "Good grief, I have no idea why people would risk it. Says here its poison is 1,200 times more deadly than cyanide. It's so powerful, a lethal dose is smaller than the head of a pin."

Goldie came over and sprawled out at my feet with a content sigh, Gator tucked into her mouth for safekeeping.

Thank heavens. My elbow was getting sore.

"Wouldn't all four judges have been poisoned then?" Willow asked.

Mallory scanned the screen. "Well, apparently there's also pufferfish that aren't poisonous, so you can eat those without dropping dead." She stretched out her legs on the sofa and rebalanced her laptop. "Pufferfish caught off the east coast of Florida are potentially poisonous, so you're not supposed to eat those. But the ones caught from the mid-Atlantic coastal waters don't have the deadly toxin, so those are safe. It all depends on their diet."

"That's a lot of trusting the source on where the fish came from," I said. I'm not sure I'd take that gamble.

"That's the big question, isn't it?" Willow stood up from the chair and stretched her back. "With all the restaurants' lies Ruth Russo was digging up, how could she ever trust a restaurant owner to serve her pufferfish in the first place? A fish that could potentially kill her. I'd have to pass."

I nodded. "Agreed. That's exactly what Ruth Russo was doing, too. Eroding the public's trust in local restaurants. Bet the restaurant owners who knew what she was up to were just fit to be tied. Like I said... good motive for murder."

CHAPTER FIVE

"There you go, Mr. Palmer, all set." I handed the receipt for twenty cans of Premium Star cat food over to the stooped man across the counter. Darwin's Pet Boutique was surprisingly busy this morning for it being summer and all. Thank the stars Mallory was here to help out. I hated to make our elderly customers stand in line. "Mallory can carry this out to your car for you."

Mr. Palmer's watery gray eyes shone behind thick glasses as he situated the weighted-down, cotton shopping bag on his shoulder. "Not necessary, young lady. It's my exercise for the day. See you in two weeks."

"All right then, you give Midget and Molly a good scratch from me." I moved my attention to the next customer, a woman who bore a startling resemblance to Goldie Hawn. "Hey there, Susan, find everything you need?"

Susan placed her items on the counter with a bright, movie star smile. "Yep. Though I really should've thought to book Sassy with Sylvia before she left. Her bangs are out of control. When does that lucky lady get back from traipsing around Europe?"

I scanned the bag of bully sticks, canine dental gel and paw soother balm. The balm had been a big hit, as the hot Florida sidewalks are hard on a dog's paw pads. "She comes back to work September 3rd. I can check her schedule, but she's pretty booked up when she returns. Charlie's doing what she calls *pawdicures* while Sylvia's out. She trims their nails and paints them. Also, aromatherapy baths if you'd like to at least get Sassy in for that."

Susan's blue eyes sparkled. "Well, heck, forget Sassy, book *me* for that!" We shared a laugh as she handed me her credit card.

"All right let's do both." I held up a hand with a grin. "Not book you both. I mean put Sassy on Sylvia's schedule for as soon as she's available and see if Charlie has an opening for her tomorrow."

As I finished up her order, my phone vibrated under the counter. I took a quick peek. It was Will. "Here you go." I handed Susan the receipt to sign. "And give me a sec to check with Charlie about tomorrow." While I walked back to the grooming room, I listened to the message Will had left.

"Darwin, give me a call back as soon as you can. We're holding Hana Ishida, the owner of Happi Sushi, for questioning in Ruth Russo's death. She had her dog with her in the car when we picked her up. I'd like to avoid taking it to the shelter."

After Charlie put Sassy on her schedule for tomorrow, I returned Will's call. "Hey, of course, I'll come get her dog. The dachshund, right?"

"Thanks. Yeah, but I'm actually close by so I can drop her off."

"Okay. See you soon."

Mallory plopped a bag of aquarium gravel on the counter and moved around to ring up her customer.

I leaned in close to her ear. "Will's coming to drop off Hana Ishida's dachshund. He's holding Hana for questioning in Ruth Russo's death."

Mallory glanced sharply at me. "She's the one who served the pufferfish?"

"Possibly. I'll see what I can find out when he gets here."

Will pushed through the door ten minutes later with Daisy trailing reluctantly behind him on a leash.

"Hey!" I raced over to them. Then remembering how unsure Daisy was when I'd met her at the seafood festival, I kept my distance and talked softly instead. "Hey, girl, it's gonna be all right. You're safe here and we have yummy treats."

Goldie trotted up and began sniffing the new arrival, tail wagging with excitement. Daisy sat her rump down and took in the shop with her head low, long ears hanging.

"I don't think she wants to play right now, Goldie." I grabbed Goldie's collar and pulled her away, giving Daisy some space. "So, Hana, huh? She didn't really seem like the type to poison someone," I whispered to Will.

He handed me the end of Daisy's leash. Daisy lifted her head and watched me. "She was the only one who served pufferfish to the judges. The tox screen came back, it was definitely Tetrodotoxin poisoning or TTX for short. And there's a history between her and Ruth Russo. Happi Sushi is Hana's second restaurant. Russo apparently destroyed Hana's first restaurant, Kabuto Grill in Tampa, with a blistering review." He rubbed the back of his neck roughly. "Anyway, there are some things that don't add up. Like why the other judges weren't poisoned, too. The prosecutor feels we have enough to hold her for questioning and get a search warrant but not charges. Hopefully the search warrant for Happi Sushi comes through. We have to release her by Wednesday but wanted to bring her in before she could hide any possible evidence."

I kept an eye on Daisy but didn't react when she came over to sniff my sandaled feet. "Well, just so you know, we looked up pufferfish last night, and they're only poisonous if they come from certain areas. So, Hana could've thought she was serving safe fish."

"Yeah, that's one possibility. I'll know more when I interview her in a bit." He shifted his weight to the other leg and glanced at a nearby customer.

"What is it?" I asked, crossing my arms.

He leaned in closer to me. "Let me know if you... you know... get anything from Daisy."

"Oh." I wasn't expecting that. "Okay, I will." I glanced down at Daisy. She'd sprawled out at my feet, brown eyes staring sadly off in the distance. "I hope for this girl's sake, Hana is innocent."

"Me too." Will squeezed my arms and planted a kiss on my forehead. "Thanks for taking her for now. Call you later."

Willow walked up and stood beside me, staring at Daisy. "Poor thing. Her life may have just changed forever, and she has no idea. Want me to take her for a walk?"

"Sure." I handed over the leash. Then, bending down and bracing myself, I reached out and stroked her glossy, black coat. There was a light tingle up my arm, a feeling of confusion and leather car seats that I recognized as Will's sedan. Nothing useful. I scratched under her ear, and she lifted her head to look at me, her long, narrow mouth closed tight. She didn't trust me yet.

"Anything?" Mallory asked.

I shook my head. "She's confused. Nothing to give us a clue what happened, though."

"Will better figure it out soon," Mallory said. "Or this girl's photo is going to end up on our bulletin board of dogs that need a home."

"Speakin' of, do you want to take a ride with me tonight? I promised Frankie I'd check out a property she found as a possible site for the Peter Vanek Animal Shelter."

"Sure." Mallory's mouth curved into a mischievous smile. "Unless I have something better to do, like a date with Brad."

I bit my tongue, refusing to take the bait.

The lull was over as the next wave of customers began filtering in. Being busy did make the day fly by and before I knew it, I was flipping the sign to 'Closed' and locking the door. When I walked back to the counter to start on the register, my phone was vibrating.

"Hey, Will."

"Hey, listen, I have a proposition for you. I've gotta check out a restaurant owner's alibi and thought we could grab dinner at his restaurant. What do you say? Pick you up in an hour?"

I bit my lip. Besides really wanting to see Will, I was curious how it went with Hana today. "I was supposed to check out some property tonight for the shelter, but I guess that can wait 'til tomorrow."

※   ※   ※

When I opened my bedroom door, I expected to see Daisy curled up in Goldie's dog bed, but it was empty.

Goldie pushed past me into the room and started sniffing around. Her nose took her to her bed, but then under mine and around the white comforter lying in a heap on the floor.

"Daisy," I called. "Where are you, girl?" I followed Goldie as she sniffed her way to the pile of clean clothes in the corner that I hadn't bothered to hang up yet.

Goldie shoved her nose into the pile and then pawed at something.

That's when I saw two brown eyes and a long snout poking out of the sleeve of my favorite pink, cotton sweater. Lifting up a pair of yoga pants, I spotted her tail wagging out the other end. A burst of laughter escaped me. "What in the world are you doing in there?"

Daisy tried to maneuver herself toward me, but only ended up rolling onto her back. Her tail wagged harder.

"Are you stuck?" Tugging on the sleeve didn't work. I ended up pulling the sweater back over her head, unsheathing her. She shook her body, her ears flapping comically around her head. Her thin whip-like tail swished back and forth twice. I kissed the top of her head. Guess we're friends now. "You're welcome. Now come on, let's get you some dinner."

After I fed the dogs—and bribed Mallory to take them out—I ran back upstairs and threw on a sundress, ran a brush through my short waves, swiped on some lip gloss and then hurried back downstairs. I'd texted Will and asked if the restaurant was dog-friendly and it was, so I was bringing Goldie.

"Don't forget to find out if Will thinks Hana is really guilty," Mallory said as I headed for the elevator with Goldie in tow.

"Hana who?" I teased her. She narrowed her eyes at me. I laughed. "You know me, of course I'll ask."

CHAPTER SIX

We were seated outside on the wooden deck at Skippy's Seafood House, next to the bar. Boats were anchored in the water around the dock and fans twirled on high above us, bravely battling the summer heat and humidity. Our waiter, "Jim from NY," brought out a bowl of water for Goldie. He set it down beneath our tall table where she lay watching silvery snook glide along the cement seawall below us.

"This place is pretty dead for being on the water," I whispered.

As the hostess had walked us through the dining room, there'd only been one family and one elderly couple. Out here on the deck there were two lone women at the bar, huddled over margaritas.

Will glanced around at the empty tables. "Apparently this place was on the receiving end of one of Ms. Russo's scathing reviews six months back and hasn't recovered yet. The owner, Skip Pascoe, is one of the suspects St. Pete PD has on their radar for some threats against Russo."

"Like death threats?" I asked.

Will took a sip of his water, then nodded. "There was an envelope sent to her office at the St. Pete Journal right after the review, with a pretty specific threat. The threats have been escalating over time. The last one came with her car window busted out and a load of dead fish dumped in her car."

I grimaced. "Yuck. Can't imagine that smell would be easy to get out."

"No, but the real problem is, where'd someone get that many dead fish?"

I squeezed lemon into my water. "Probably need to own a boat or a restaurant that buys fish in bulk."

Will nodded, closing his menu. "It was local fish, so most likely a boat owner."

Jim from NY had been lurking nearby, obviously itching for something to do. When he saw Will close the menu, he rushed over. "Are we ready to order?"

We gave him our order and then Will asked, "Is Skip here tonight? I'd like a word with him."

Jim finished writing on his pad. "Sure, I'll get him for you."

A few minutes later, a short stocky man in a Hawaiian shirt and dirty apron came through the doors. He had a white beard and mustache, his face ruddy with sun, hard work and possibly alcohol abuse.

He held his hand out to Will. "Skip Pascoe, what can I do for y'all?" His speech held the long, drawn-out lilt of the deep south. His accent was even more pronounced than mine. Louisiana, if I had to guess.

We both shook Skip's damp hand, then Will pulled out his badge and dropped it on the table. I watched the man's face turn a deeper shade of red. His light blue eyes flicked back up to Will with suspicion and heat. He folded his arms above his belly and rocked back on his heels. "Well, then, what can I do for ya, *Detective*?"

Will smiled slightly. "Do you own a boat, Mr. Pascoe?"

The man's hand reached up and stroked his beard. "I do. Is that illegal now?"

Will's smile stretched a bit, but I could see the calculation behind his eyes. "Nah. In fact, I was just telling my girlfriend how nice it must be to own a boat around here. I hear the fishing's good, and that this month's been good for trout, redfish and snook in particular."

Skip Pascoe cocked his head, his tone heavy with suspicion. "That's right."

Will leaned back in his chair. "Catch any yourself this month?"

Skip Pascoe shifted on his feet and glanced down at Will's badge. "Sure, I reckon I have."

Will held his smile as he asked, "Enough to fill a car?"

Understanding lit up Skip's eyes and then they narrowed. "I see what you're getting' at, Detective. I've already told the police I ain't had nothin' to do with that woman's car being filled with fish."

"But you did have a problem with Ruth Russo. Because she gave your restaurant a bad review, right?"

His ears reddened. "Not just a bad review. She called me a liar. Snuck out samples of our Florida Blue Crab and had them tested. Wrote that we were conning our customers."

"Was she right?"

Skip's anger deflated. "Look, I'll admit we should'a just called it lump crab or something, since most of the time it comes from Vietnam or Indonesia, but what's the difference? Everyone does it. And it is crab. Not like it's chicken we're calling crab. It's crab!"

Will picked up his badge while maintaining eye contact with Skip. "Guess you'd be happy to learn that Ms. Russo is deceased then?"

"Dead?" Skip's white, caterpillar-like brows shot up. "So, she *was* poisoned at the seafood festival?"

Will nodded, still watching him closely.

"Huh." He glanced out at a fishing boat cruising by. "Well, can't say I'll lose any sleep over it. If that's a crime, arrest me."

Will leaned forward, resting his forearms on the table. "So, you were at the festival all day on Sunday?"

Skip rubbed his forehead and sighed. "Sure. Had a booth for the restaurant. Was there until they shut down the whole thing."

Will took out a card and handed it to him. "I'd like you to call and make an appointment to come talk to me at the station. Bring your lawyer if you like."

Skip Pascoe's nostrils flared as he took it. "'Bout her death?"

"I just need a more detailed statement of your movements at the festival. Look at it as an opportunity to get yourself off the suspect list."

Skip took the card with a huff. "I can save you some trouble. I had nothin' to do with her death."

"Still. I'd like to continue this conversation at the station." Will and Skip stared at each other for a long moment before Skip finally pursed his lips, nodded and then turned away.

"Mr. Pascoe," Will called. When he turned back, Will said, "Sooner rather than later."

"What do you think?" I asked after Skip pushed back through the doors.

Will tapped his fingers on the table. "I'm thinking I need to get a writing sample from Mr. Pascoe to see if it matches the note that was left in Ruth Russo's car."

"Well, hopefully he'll come in soon." I watched two pelicans glide over the water in tandem. "What about Hana Ishida? Did you talk to her today?"

He waited for Jim to set our plates down and fill up our water glasses. "Thanks."

"Get you folks anything else right now?"

Will gave him a distracted smile. "We're good." After Jim left, Will picked up his fork. "I did. Hana admitted to blaming Russo for losing her Tampa restaurant, which she apparently took pretty hard. But she's maintaining her innocence. Says the pufferfish she served the judges came from a trusted source and was harvested in the mid-Atlantic. The warrant came through, and we did find pufferfish at Happi Sushi during the search this afternoon. Samples are at the lab now on a rush order for DNA testing, so we'll know soon if she's telling the truth."

I finished swallowing a bite of my grouper. The food was really good here, shame they'd lost their customers. But I had to admit, knowing they'd lied about their crab made me suspicious if my meal was actually fresh grouper. The seeds of doubt had been planted.

I wiped at my mouth with a cloth napkin. "It does make sense that it would've been a ticked off restaurant owner, but it doesn't make a lick of sense that Ruth Russo was the only judge who was poisoned, does it? I mean, unless Hana had cooked up some toxic pufferfish, too, and only served that to Ruth Russo, giving the other judges the safe fish. That seems like an awful lot of trouble to go through."

"You'd be surprised the lengths people will go to for revenge." Will stabbed at his shrimp Caesar salad. "Unfortunately, the only thing that would convince me of Ms. Ishida's innocence right now, since she had both motive and opportunity, is if we found evidence Russo ingested the toxin in something other than the pufferfish Ms. Ishida served her."

"Pufferfish toxin in something other than the pufferfish? That's kind of unlikely, isn't it?"

"It's a long shot, yeah." Will set his fork down and leaned back. "You can't just buy TTX off the street. It's heavily regulated. You'd need a medical license to purchase it from a supplier. That's also why this couldn't have been an accidental poisoning." He shrugged. "We just have to link Hana Ishida to the toxin to officially charge her." He glanced around and then leaned forward. "How's her dog holding up? Did you... see anything helpful?"

I shook my head. "Unfortunately, no. Just a bit of confusion when she was in your car."

Goldie backed out of her spot beneath the table and rested her chin on my leg. I broke off a piece of my fish and gave it to her. It was gone in a millisecond, and she was licking her chops for more. I stroked her head instead. "There was that argument I saw the first time I touched Daisy, remember? The smashed glass bowl? But I don't see how that could have anything to do with Ruth Russo's death."

Will thought for a moment and then shook his head. "I don't either. But only because we don't have enough information. I'd need to know what the argument was about."

I ran back through the vision in my head but didn't see any way it helped. "Speaking of Daisy, think you could ask Hana if we could grab some of Daisy's food from her place?"

"I'll ask. Though, if she does have something to hide, I'm not sure she'll want us in her house."

CHAPTER SEVEN

When I arrived home, Grandma Winters was just pulling something out of the oven that smelled like cinnamon buns. She greeted me with a wave as I slipped off my shoes. Petey scrambled out of the kitchen, tripped and bowled into my feet.

Shaking my head, I scooped him up and let him frantically lick and bite my ears. "Well, aren't you lookin' adorable tonight." Mallory had him dressed in a white onesie with blue bears.

Speaking of Mallory, I noticed her, along with Willow and Goldie, standing at the French doors, staring out at the balcony.

I sidled up beside them, noting the half-grimace, half-smirk on my sisters' faces. "What's going—" My mouth dropped as I spotted what had them so amused. "Oh no." I handed Petey off to Mallory and cracked open the French door, so Goldie didn't follow me as I slipped out.

"Oh, Daisy." I moaned as I stared at the potting soil spread all over the balcony. Daisy was on her back, happily rolling around in it. Picking my way through the dirt in my bare feet, I lifted the torn, empty bag and placed it in the trash can. The mess could wait until morning, but I really hoped Daisy liked baths.

Willow opened the door for me as I held Daisy against my chest, beneath her armpits. Mallory had lost interest and was talking to someone on the phone.

"Watch out, girl," I said, moving Goldie out of the way with my knee as she sniffed Daisy.

Turned out, Daisy loved baths. I returned twenty minutes later with a cleaned-up Daisy and a fresh t-shirt. Daisy raced around the living room, rubbing her face on the furniture and crème shag rug beneath the coffee table. Goldie grabbed her ball on a rope and pranced after Daisy, trying to get her to play.

I plopped down on the loveseat, my lower back aching from leaning over the tub. "Who was that?" I asked.

Mallory had just finished her conversation and sat up, moving Petey to a pillow by her side. "Oh, that was Brad Rose." Leaning forward, she picked her laptop up off the coffee table. "We're going to hang out tomorrow after work. But more importantly, I found something real interesting you have to see."

Reluctantly, I pushed my tired bones up and went to sit beside her. Lucky crossed the back of the sofa to rub her side against my hair, purring. Her tail curled around my head, and I had to push it out of my face. Then I reached up to give her the attention she demanded.

Mallory's fingers moved expertly over the keyboard. "I got bored and googled Hana Ishida while you were gone. Check this out. This was a few months ago." She pressed play on a YouTube video and angled the screen toward me.

I recognized Hana, her long dark hair in a ponytail, her arms crossed in front of her thin frame. She was being interviewed by a young woman with a rainbow mohawk.

"I'm here with Hana Ishida who has just opened Happy Sushi here on 2nd street. Can you tell us a bit about your new place?" She held the microphone in front of Hana's face.

Hana stared into the camera; her gray-green eyes dull and sad. "We specialize in fresh sushi and sashimi for reasonable price."

"You came here from Tampa, where you owned Kabuto Grill, a higher-end Japanese restaurant. Why did you close that location last year?"

Hana's small frame visibly stiffened. "It was not by choice. It was panned by a no-talent critic, Ruth Russo. She destroyed my restaurant with her viciousness." Tears pooled in her eyes, making them shine. "I lost everything. It's a good thing she doesn't show her face. If I find out who she is, I have a special fugu dish just for her."

The interviewer laughed nervously.

My hand went to my mouth. Mallory pressed pause. The video stopped on an image of Hana's face. Her expression was tight with pain, and tears blurred her eyes.

"A fugu dish just for her?" I whispered. "That sounds like a threat. And the seafood festival was the first time Ruth Russo revealed her identity in public. Had Hana been plotting her revenge for a year?"

Mallory's hand moved to Petey, resting protectively on his back. "It's not looking good for Daisy's mom. You should send this link to Will."

I glanced over at Daisy, who was happily chewing a bully stick next to Goldie. "Yeah, good idea."

Grandma Winters padded softly into the room and handed me a cup of tea. "Drink this and then it's time for me to help you practice."

"Oh, right now?" I was dog tired and not sure I'd be able to drum up the level of concentration required, but I wasn't about to argue with Grandma Winters, either. I accepted the cup of lavender-scented tea.

❖ ❖ ❖

Grandma Winters sat across from me in my practice room, a glass bowl full of collected rainwater in the middle of the coffee table. Around the glass bowl she'd placed my ocean gems and jasper. The only lighting in the room was the two white candles burning at both ends of the table.

"Are you going to show me how to tap into Universal Consciousness?" I asked. This was the one thing I hadn't been able to do yet, and I knew from my sisters that it was the one thing necessary to have complete control and unlimited power over my gift.

Her hands were folded in her lap. A serene energy emanated from her. "Tonight we'll just work on your foundation. Breathe and set your intention first."

I closed my eyes, feeling a bit irritated at her taking me back to the basics. "I have been practicing a little," I mumbled.

"Still your mind." Her voice was a sharp command.

I took a deep breath in through my nose and filled my lungs, then followed the air with my attention as I blew it out slowly through my mouth. I repeated this ritual until I felt my shoulders fall away from my ears and saw the empty blue sky bloom in the darkness, my symbolic image of a clear mind. From here, I seated myself in the center of my being.

"Good. Now open your eyes and focus on the water." Grandma Winter's voice was barely a whisper now.

Opening my eyes, I expanded my attention, reaching out with my energy like an extended, invisible finger to the water in the bowl. It was almost euphoric, the pulsing power I felt when I connected. The water molecules began to dance, bouncing off each other as my energy excited them.

"Remain in control. Let's try clockwise first," Grandma Winters whispered.

Keeping my breathing steady, I steered the water smoothly in a clockwise direction. As I picked up speed, it hollowed out in the center, the walls of water lifting out of the bowl.

"Now, switch directions without losing a drop from the bowl."

Keeping laser-like focus, I slowed down the water's speed, letting it settle back into the bowl before I reversed its direction. My head was beginning to ache from the heavy concentration, but I was doing it. I was in control. That is, until I suddenly felt a sharp pinch on my arm.

"Ouch!" I squealed, breaking my focus. The water sloshed out of the bowl and puddled on the table. I stared at Grandma Winters as I rubbed my forearm. "You pinched me."

She was settling back on the zafu cushion with a frown. "You must not lose control because of a little pain."

My eyes widened as I realized the implications of her words. "You expect this rescue mission to be… painful?"

Her expression softened, but her eyes burned in the candlelight. "We expect the best, prepare for the worst."

I rubbed my arm and lowered my eyes to the spilled water. "I haven't really thought about how dangerous this could be."

"That is why I asked Zach to go with you, even though I'd rather he not be in your life."

I lifted my head at the concern in her voice. "He would never hurt me."

Her frown deepened. "No, not on purpose. But I can't see Will putting up with his attachment to you forever. Can you?"

I stared at her. It was the first time she'd brought up Will. And she was right. Zach was an obstacle in our relationship, whether I tried to convince myself we were just friends or not. All the energy drained from my body and a dull ache pulsed in my temples.

CHAPTER EIGHT

Frankie came through the doors as soon as we opened the pet boutique, her eyes bloodshot, her hair sticking up like a threatened porcupine.

I was kneeling on the floor unpacking a large aquarium we'd special ordered. "Rough night?" Pushing the box aside, I stood and hugged her. "Is it the hot flashes?" She'd been complaining lately about the hot flashes, insomnia and forgetfulness of menopause, often repeating her favorite joke: She knows she's forgotten something but can't remember what it is.

After giving me a limp hug, Frankie shuffled over in her bedroom slippers to sit at the table. "Worse. It's Spider. He overdosed last night."

My hand flew to my mouth. "Oh no. Is he... alive?"

"He's at St. Anthony's. In a coma." She dropped her head into her hands.

"That's awful. I'm so sorry." I filled an infuser with some soothing vanilla lemongrass tea leaves, then poured hot water over it from the electric kettle. "Here you go."

She wrapped her hands around the hot cup. Her red, swollen eyes met mine. "I just don't get it. He's not working yet. I've been giving him just the necessities. Nothing he could sell. Mac's been helping me keep an eye on him. Whenever Spider would leave Pirate City, Mac sent someone with him. So, where'd he get the money for heroin?"

"Where there's a will, there's a way, I guess." I sighed. "Is there anything we can do for him?"

"Right now, the doctor says it's a wait and see situation."

I squeezed Frankie's hand. "Hey, you're not blaming yourself, are you?"

Her bottom lip quivered. "I feel like I failed him."

"Oh, Frankie." I wiggled her hand so she'd look at me. When she finally did, I gave her my most sincere look. "You did everything you could. It's not your fault."

"My head knows that, but my heart is broken."

※　※　※

At lunchtime Will picked me and Daisy up from the boutique. We headed over to Hana's place, as she'd agreed to let us enter her home to get some of Daisy's things. I wanted to believe that meant she had nothing to hide. Will still wasn't convinced.

I angled the air vent toward me, enjoying the exceptionally cool air in Will's sedan. The temperature had hit 92 degrees, and the sun blazed down on St. Pete through a cloudless sky. As my mom would say, you could fry an egg on the sidewalk. "So, how's Hana holdin' up?"

Will made a right turn onto 34th street. Traffic was heavy for summertime, though it was lunchtime so that probably accounted for it. "Fine under the circumstances. She seems more angry than anything else. And worried about Daisy. I assured her Daisy's in good hands."

"Yeah, Daisy is the last thing she should be worried about." I tensed as the driver in front of us hit their brakes hard. "Did you ask her about that YouTube interview where she threatened to serve Ruth Russo a fugu dish?"

Will checked his side mirror and moved to the middle lane. "I did. She said of course she was upset when she lost Kabuto Grill because of Russo. But denied actually planning on poisoning her."

"Do you believe her?"

He glanced at me, but I couldn't see his expression behind his sunglasses. "Honestly, no. I think Hana probably had a pretty specific fantasy that ended with her serving Russo her last meal. Whether she'd go through with it in real life or not is the question."

I thought about this as we drove out of the suburbs of St. Pete through the gates of Paradise Trailer Park and made a left onto Orange Blossom Street. The narrow blacktop road stretched between rows of rectangular homes. They all looked the same with white siding and flat roofs. The outside décor was the only thing that differentiated them. Some had flowers planted in front, some had plastic chairs or lawn chairs in the small yards.

Hana's mobile home sat on a tiny plot of land just like the others. There was new dirt and mulch along the front, like she was getting ready to plant something. Will pulled the sedan under the attached awning, and I helped Daisy to the ground.

Daisy's tail wagged hopefully as Will unlocked the door. She pushed past my legs with a little whine and scurried into the house. The air conditioner and lights had been left on. Daisy turned in circles, sniffing the tile floor in the kitchen—which was actually high-end for a trailer, sporting black and gold marble countertops and stainless steel appliances—and then the living room and finally down the squat hall to what I assumed was Hana's bedroom.

"Poor thing is lookin' for Hana," I said. Walking into the kitchen, I began opening the cabinets, searching for Daisy's food. Beneath the sink there was a small garbage can. Shards of the glass bowl from my vision lay on top of other trash. "Hey, Will," I called.

He appeared beside me as I balanced on the balls of my feet. "What's up?"

I tipped the trash can so he could see inside. "That argument I told you I saw when I touched Daisy... the one where someone threw a glass bowl at the wall. Well, it must've been recent because this is the bowl."

"Guess we know it was definitely Hana involved in the argument. And Ogden Stewart, by the shoe size."

I pushed the garbage can back in place and stood. "Yeah. Maybe Hana told him what she was planning, and he got upset?" I glanced around. "Though, I'm squashing my own hope here that Hana had nothing to do with Ruth Russo's death."

Daisy padded into the kitchen, a small red rubber ball in her mouth. She dropped it at my feet.

I gently kicked it, and she chased it under the dining room table.

Will was still thinking about what I'd said. "I guess it wouldn't hurt to bring Ogden in and talk to him about Hana's state of mind before the seafood festival. She did admit that she knew beforehand Russo was going to be one of the judges."

I nudged him with my elbow. "Plus, you could ask for his autograph."

A deep chuckle resonated in Will's chest. "I don't think that would be appropriate."

But I could tell he liked the idea by his lingering smile. "All right. Let's find your food, Daisy." I continued my search until I found a bag of dry food in the pantry. "Here we are." Daisy dropped the ball and looked up at me hopefully. "Hungry?" I spotted her stainless-steel bowls and added a few scoops along with fresh water. Then I leaned against the counter and eyed Will. "While she eats, you could take a peek around... see if you spot anything suspicious."

Will stared down the hall. "Believe me, I'd love to. But anything I find without a warrant would be inadmissible anyway."

"You're such a rule-follower," I teased. I guess that was one thing Will and I had in common. The exact opposite of Zach. I turned away, angry at myself.

Stop comparing Will to Zach.

When Daisy had finished eating, I tossed her bowls and rubber ball in a shopping bag, grabbed her food and we headed out. Will was in a hurry to get back to the station for his interview with Skip Pascoe.

CHAPTER NINE

Mallory was leaning her elbows on the counter and squinting at her phone when I walked into the boutique. Willow was there, too, helping Marco, a regular customer with a blue and yellow macaw named Captain Hook parked on his shoulder. The parrot was a local celebrity during tourist season, when people paid five bucks a pop to get their picture taken with him.

I waved. "Hey, y'all."

"Hell-o," Captain Hook said. Then he went into his routine of whistling, yodeling and calling himself a "pretty bird".

I giggled as Goldie followed me to the counter, her head turning to keep an eye on the large bird. "Good thing my dog can't talk like that." I bumped Mallory with my hip to move her over so I could shove my straw bag under the counter.

"How'd it go?" Mallory asked, without pulling her attention from the phone.

"Good, we found Daisy's food. I stashed her upstairs to take a nap in my bedroom." I eyed Mallory's scrunched up nose and narrowed eyes. "What's up?"

She tapped her lip. "I found Ruth Russo's Twitter account. The woman is... *was* brutal with the restaurants she visited. But the worst part was reading her last few Tweets from the festival. Here, have a look." She angled her phone toward me and I read:

Round 1 Golden Lobster Contest. Asian sea trout. Cabbage slaw? Interesting choice. Not. #stpete #seafoodfestival (a photo of the meal accompanied the text)

To the guy in the red hat staring at me, take a picture it lasts longer. #creep #getalife #seafoodfestival

For all you do? Thank you anonymous donor. #favoritewine #Chateau Ste.Veuve (photo of plastic cup with blurred bottle in background)

Round 4 Golden Lobster Contest. Chef's choice. Pufferfish? Lol #ManyEnemies #hopeitsnotthetoxickind (photo of pufferfish dish)

"Well that's downright creepy," I whispered. "She didn't even know how right she was about the pufferfish." A chill raised the hairs on the back of my neck. "And that Tweet about the guy in the red hat staring at her. I noticed a guy in a red baseball hat staring as the paramedics carried her away. I even snapped a photo of him. I wonder if it's the same guy?" I dug my phone out of my bag and pulled up the photo. "See how he's standing there smirkin'?"

Mallory took the phone and enlarged the photo of his face. "That is suspicious. Maybe Will can find out who he is." She handed me back my phone. "Anyway, mind if I skedaddle about an hour early today? Brad wants to take me to that Japanese place where they cook the food in front of you. It gets crowded after six."

I felt the muscles in my body tighten protectively, but I tried not to show it. "Yeah sure. No problem. So, y'all are just going to dinner then?"

Mallory crossed her arms over her green spaghetti-strap top. "I can take care of myself you know. I'm not a child."

Yes, you are a child. I bit my tongue and smiled at her instead. "You're right. I'd still appreciate a text if you go anywhere afterwards."

She rolled her eyes. "Fine." Then scooped up Petey from his gated-in play area & grabbed two leashes. "I'm taking the dogs to the park. I need some air. Come on, Goldie."

As she left, Frankie walked back in. She'd combed her hair and had real shoes on. Goldie and her two Chihuahuas greeted each other with their usual butt-sniffing session before Mallory led Goldie away.

"Hey, Frankie." I dug two small sweet potato treats from the jar on the counter and handed one to each of her dogs. They crunched them with their tiny jaws and then hoovered up the crumbs they dropped. "So glad to see Itty's feelin' better. Any news on Spider?"

Frankie dropped her bag under the table and hoisted herself up on the bar chair. "No news on Spider. I'm going crazy, I just have to keep myself distracted. Tell me what's going on in your world."

I walked over, keeping an eye on the elderly couple talking at the edge of the cat food aisle, in case they needed help. "Well, I'm still dog-sitting Daisy while Hana's being held for questioning."

Frankie's voice held a touch of surprise. "Will still thinks Hana's the one who poisoned Ruth Russo, huh?"

I rubbed the tension out of my stiff neck. "He can't rule her out yet."

Itty and Bitty suddenly noticed Captain Hook as Marco rounded the end of the bird and reptile aisle. The sound of scrambling nails on the floor and high-pitched barking ensued. Captain Hook bobbed his head and barked back at them. The two dogs turned tail, darting under the table to hide behind Frankie's large leather bag.

Sharing an amused glance with Marco, Frankie then turned back to me. "I have two chickens in dog suits. Anyway, you were sayin'?"

I rested an elbow on the table. "That he can't rule Hana out yet. They're waiting for the tests to come back on the blowfish found at her restaurant—and the samples they found at the seafood festival—to see if it was the toxic kind. There's another suspect, too, though. Skip Pascoe, who owns Skippy's Seafood House. The police think he was sending death threats to Ruth Russo. Will's interviewing him today."

"I know Skip. He has a temper, but I can't see him actually killin' someone." Steam rose up between us as Frankie poured hot water over a tea infuser, releasing the scent of cinnamon and cloves. "Besides, they say poison is a woman's weapon of choice."

"Do they?" I thought back to Hana's interview on YouTube. She did allude to poisoning Ruth Russo. I also recalled the argument I'd witnessed between her and Ogden at the seafood festival.

"Hana does seem really angry. Anyway, I hope to high heaven I don't have to find a new home for Daisy. She's such a sweet girl. Doesn't deserve to have her world turned upside down like that."

Frankie lifted her cup. "Speakin' of finding dogs homes, sugar, have you had a chance to take a look at that property I found for the shelter? I'd like to put in an offer on it asap."

"Sorry, I haven't." I slid out of the chair. The elderly couple were glancing around like they needed help. "I'll do it tonight."

"How about I pick you up after closing? Drive you out there?"

"Sure, let's do it," I said.

❖ ❖ ❖

After Frankie dropped me back off at the house, I settled in to chat with Grandma Winters and Willow. We got comfy in the living room, each balancing a piece of homemade cherry strudel and a cup of tea. This was the only thing Grandma Winters did that seemed like something a human grandmother would do... she loved to bake. Though, considering she used some magick to whip up these desserts, I'm not sure using the word "bake" was appropriate.

Goldie and Daisy were playing a game of tug with a rubber pull toy. Goldie would let Daisy win, then Daisy would trot around with the toy all proud before Goldie would grab it and start the game over. Petey had given up joining in after getting knocked down a few times and now watched the game from his hiding place beneath the coffee table.

It had been a good day. No fires to put out at the pet boutique, and the property Frankie had found for the future Peter Vanek Animal Shelter seemed perfect and within our budget. She was going to put in the offer tomorrow.

Halfway through my piece of strudel, the day took a turn for the worse. Mallory stumbled out of the elevator in tears and ran up the stairs without a word to any of us.

We all shared a stunned look.

"Well that's not good," Willow finally said.

Grandma Winters nodded at me, a knowing look on her face. "Darwin, you should go talk to her."

I knocked softly on the bedroom door. "Mal?" No answer. I knocked harder. Lucky meowed at my feet. She'd beat me to the closed door.

"Go away!" Mallory croaked.

"I'm not going away. And you know how stubborn I can be." There was no answer, so I tried the door. It opened.

Lucky padded in and gracefully hopped onto the bed.

Mallory lay sprawled out on the yellow comforter with peach seashells, her face buried in a pillow. Her shoulders shook with sobs.

My heart ached. I hurried over, collapsing onto the bed next to her. "Oh, Mal. What happened?"

She rolled over but kept her forearm over her eyes. It didn't cover her blotchy, tear-stained cheeks. "I'm a freak! I'm a freak, and I'll never be able to have a normal relationship. I hate our magick!"

I stroked the damp hair off her forehead. "I know you don't mean that. Tell me what happened."

She removed her arm and stared up at the ceiling. The skin around her eyes was puffy and pink.

Lucky headbutted her, purring.

Mallory reached out and stroked the cat's back. "There was this girl sittin' on the other side of Brad at the table. She kept flirting with him. I don't know whether he was just being polite or was really interested in her, but he didn't discourage her. It was so painful. It actually hurt my chest to watch her head so close to his as they whispered to each other. I just lost it." She groaned. "The chef was cooking, and I couldn't control it. I didn't mean to connect to the fire... but I did. It blew up and leapt toward them. Brad's shirt sleeve actually caught on fire."

Her eyes met mine, and I could see the fear still lurking there. Fear of her own power and the loss of control. I understood completely. I squeezed her hand. "What did Brad do?"

"He jumped up and yelled. I tossed my glass of water on him. The fire went out, but it had burned him. His arm was actually red." A moan escaped her lips. "I hurt him, Darwin." The tears fell fresh. "I couldn't even face him after that. I just ran out."

I struggled to keep my own tears in check. Now I knew why Grandma Winters sent me up here. "You know, the same thing happened to me at the seafood festival."

Mallory flicked her eyes back to mine. "Really?"

I cringed, remembering the scene. "Will's ex-wife was there. She's real pretty and was actin' like she was still interested in Will. She's apparently moved back to St. Pete. When she invited him over to her place, I kind of sloshed water from her cup all over her silk top. Not on purpose. I lost control just like you. Jealousy is a powerful emotion."

Mallory's mouth twitched. She almost smiled, then she moved her gaze back to the ceiling fan twirling lazily above us. "But you didn't hurt her."

"Well, no... but you didn't hurt Brad either, not on purpose anyway. So, don't beat yourself up, okay? The thing you have to do now is the same thing I have to do. Practice to get control while we're feeling those strong emotions. Luckily, Grandma Winters is here to help us." I rubbed her arm. "We're not perfect, Mal. But it's our intention that matters. That's how we'll make sure we learn to control our magick."

She pushed herself up onto her elbows. "I'll practice every day."

I sighed. "Yeah, me too." Then I pulled her up off the bed. "Come on, there's a piece of cherry strudel downstairs with your name on it."

Willow scooted over on the sofa to make room for Mallory. Then she pointed at my phone on the end table. "You got a call while you were upstairs."

There was a missed call from Will. What in the world was he calling about at eight o'clock at night?

CHAPTER TEN

"Hey," I said when he picked up.

"What are you doing right now?" He asked quickly. Before I could answer he added, "I know it's late. Ogden Stewart didn't want to come to the station, but he's agreed to meet me for dinner tonight. I have an idea and need you to be there. Can I pick you up?"

"Well, sure. If you need me, I'm there." Though I had no earthly idea why he'd need me there. *Moral support?*

As we drove to Seltzer's Steakhouse, Will was unusually quiet. He also kept adjusting the air vents, mirrors, his seatbelt, barely making eye contact with me.

When he stopped at a red light, I rested my hand on his leg to get his attention. "Are you gonna tell me what's going on?"

He raked a hand over his face. When he finally looked at me, it was with a touch of guilt darkening his expression. "I have an idea, but if you're not comfortable with it, just tell me. I promise I'll understand. Okay?"

I slowly pulled my hand back. "What's your idea?"

He drove forward as the light changed, his knuckles turning white as he gripped the steering wheel. "I've been thinking about that argument, the one that resulted in the broken glass bowl. I'd like to hear Ogden's version of what happened. Since it was recent, it might give me a better idea of Hana's state of mind before the seafood festival. Did she blow up over something small? Did it have anything to do with Russo judging the contest? But, the only way for me to bring it up is to tell Ogden the truth about your visions." He snuck a glance at me. "Will that make you uncomfortable?"

I turned to stare out the window and watched the buildings go by. So, this was the reason he'd agreed to a dinner with Ogden instead of a police station interview. And why he wanted me there. My stomach cramped and, if I listened to my body, I was going to tell Will I couldn't do it. But I decided to listen to my heart. He was asking for my help, and I couldn't turn him down. "It will be uncomfortable, but I'll do it."

Will reached over and entwined our fingers. "I really hate to ask you to do something that's going to make you uncomfortable." He squeezed my hand. "It's okay. I'll interview other people in her orbit, see if I can figure out her mindset that way."

I appreciated how much he was struggling with this. That meant he understood what he was asking of me. The risk I'd be taking opening myself up to ridicule, being laughed at, called a witch, or the dozen other horrible things people in Savannah had called us over the years. When we were younger, we had very little control of our magick, so people saw things they shouldn't have. Of course, the stories grew and morphed as the gossip spread, making it even worse. This made Mom isolate us even more. So, telling someone about our gifts is just something that isn't done.

I'd play it by ear, get to know Ogden a bit during dinner and then decide how comfortable I was telling him. No pressure. "How about I let you know after dinner?"

Will loosened his grip on the steering wheel. "Okay. Ball's in your court."

The hostess led us to a table in the back where Ogden was waiting. When he stood to greet us, I swallowed hard. The man was an intimidating presence up close, about six-five with large hands that swallowed mine like I was a child. I caught a whiff of the spicy cologne I'd smelled when I'd touched Daisy the first time. The only thing that stopped my fear was his smile... it was genuine, despite Will being the one who currently had his girlfriend locked up.

"It's an honor to meet you. I'm a big fan," Will said as he shook his hand then pulled out my chair.

Ogden had a whole-hearted, deep chuckle. "Can't say the same."

Some of the tension eased from my body. The fact that he could joke about such a sore subject was a good sign. Maybe he wouldn't want me burned at the stake after all.

The waiter poured water into our glasses and said he'd give us time to look over the menu.

Will folded his hands and leaned toward Ogden. "I want you to know, my goal here is to get to the truth as quickly as possible and get Hana released if she's innocent."

Ogden's hazel eyes squinted as he studied Will. His voice was heavy with sadness as he said, "I can assure you she is innocent, Detective. It's why I agreed to talk with you. So, how can I help you prove it?"

Will took a sip of his water, contemplating. "I'd like to understand Hana's mental state when she found out Russo was going to be one of the judges. I imagine, as a fairly new restaurant in town, winning that Golden Lobster award would've gone a long way toward building her reputation."

"Sorry," I interrupted. "We saw Hana toss a replica of the award away at the festival. You looked upset. Did you give that to her?"

Pain flashed in his eyes. "You have to understand. When Hana lost Kabuto Grill, she was devastated. I mean like... suicidal. She'd never hurt somebody else, but she would hurt herself. In fact, she tried to. I found her in my garage with the car running."

A rush of strong emotional energy emanated from Ogden and washed over me. *Rage, fear?* Probably both.

Elbows resting on the table, he held out his hands. "That's why I adopted Daisy for her last Christmas. I figured if Hana had another soul she was responsible for, she'd think twice about locking herself in my garage again." Ogden paused and glanced over as the waiter approached. "No!" He bellowed as the waiter poised to set a basket of bread in the middle of the table. Ogden gripped the table and squeezed his eyes shut.

Will and I shared a startled look. The low drone of conversation around us paused.

"Sorry, sorry," Ogden choked out. "It's fine. Leave the bread. I apologize." When the waiter nodded slowly, and left with a forced smile, Ogden glanced at us sheepishly. "My doctor thinks the post-concussion syndrome has led to the beginning stages of CTE, chronic traumatic encephalopathy, though they can't say for sure 'til I'm in the ground. Sometimes I lose control of my emotions. I didn't mean to embarrass y'all."

I'm not sure what CTE is, but it sounds bad.

Will leaned back, his expression softening. "Sorry to hear you're struggling with that."

Ogden pinched the bridge of his nose then visibly worked on calming his breath. "Everyone's got something they're struggling with." He shifted in his chair. "Anyway, back to Hana. Where was I?"

"You adopted Daisy for her," Will gently reminded him.

He snapped his fingers. "Right. Daisy did keep Hana busy. But her depression only lifted after I'd helped her secure a loan on Happy Sushi. Convincing Hana that she wasn't a pariah, that she could start over, was no easy task, but she was pumped about this contest. If she'd won, the publicity would've taken so much pressure off her."

I was beginning to understand why the Golden Lobster Contest was such a big deal. "But when y'all found out Russo was going to be one of the judges at the festival..."

Ogden's face crumbled. "Yeah. I knew she didn't have a chance in Hades. I mean, Happy Sushi is holding its own, but Hana's working her tail off. I don't know how long she can keep up this pace."

We'd only considered revenge as a motive. But losing the contest because of Ruth Russo's bias against Hana was an even more compelling one.

That didn't make me feel better about Hana's innocence. "You really think Ruth Russo knew Hana held a grudge against her and wouldn't vote for her because of that?"

Ogden rubbed his chin roughly. "Well, yeah. Russo never publicly commented on all the angry interviews Hana had given after she'd lost Kabuto Grill. But Hana said some truly awful things. There's no way Russo didn't hear about it." He dropped his gaze, looking embarrassed. "That's why I had an exact replica of the Golden Lobster award made to give to Hana. I knew she'd never touch the real one. I don't know what I was thinking... just desperate I guess."

My heart contracted with his pain. I smiled softly. "You must really love her."

His hands curled into fists on the table. "I'd do anything for her... I just don't seem to know how to make her happy."

We paused the conversation while the waiter took our orders.

After he'd gone, Will picked the thread of conversation back up. "I haven't seen all the interviews, but I did see the one where Hana said she'd like to serve Russo a special fugu dish. That's poisonous pufferfish and a pretty big coincidence." Will watched Ogden carefully.

Ogden's big head hung for a moment, then his chin snapped up and he met Will's gaze with a new intensity. "You know you're right. What if someone else saw that interview... someone who hated Russo, too. What if it gave them the idea to poison her? Yeah, and they knew Hana would take the blame because she was actually serving pufferfish.

What if someone framed her? Used her to get rid of Russo?"

Will was either considering it or giving him the appearance of considering it to be polite. "Well, I guess we can entertain that possibility. It would've had to have been someone close to Hana. Someone who knew she'd be serving pufferfish to the judges at the seafood festival. And I don't think it would've been possible to replace the fish after it was cooked. It would've had to have been done beforehand."

"Someone that works in Hana's kitchen?" I offered, buttering a piece of the offending bread.

"Maybe." Will thought for a moment, then shook his head. "But then how would Hana have known to only serve that fish to Russo? And the other judges got the non-toxic version? That wouldn't make sense."

Unless Hana was in on it.

Will and I shared a look as Ogden's shoulders hunched, and his expression crumbled. He suddenly looked exhausted.

"I haven't interviewed her kitchen staff formally yet, though," Will said quickly. "So, I won't rule that out. Anyone you'd be suspicious of?"

I rested a hand on Will's knee under the table. I figure he was just trying to make Ogden feel better and appreciated his empathy.

"In fact, there is." Ogden tapped the table, his eyes narrowing. "Hana brought back most of her staff from the Kabuto Grill, the ones who didn't mind the drive in from Tampa. But the sous-chef, Ren Tanaka, he's new. Good at his job, sort of a rising star. Hana was over the moon that he'd be working under her. The guy would never look me in the eye, though. I just thought maybe he had a crush on Hana or something, but now that I think about it... he'd come from Kam's Sushi Palace, Hana's biggest rival in the area."

"What do you think that means?" Will asked.

Ogden stared at the candle lamp in the middle of the table, lost in thought for a moment. When he looked up, a new hope shone in his eyes. "What if Mr. Kam sent Tanaka there to sabotage Hana's restaurant? And that's why Tanaka could never look me in the eye. The man just has a shady vibe, ya know? In fact." He shook his index finger at us. "I'm pretty sure I remember Hana sayin' that Tanaka was the one who suggested pufferfish for the contest's main course."

The waiter appeared with our food. After he placed the steaming plates in front of us and left, Will said, "Okay, if that's true, that's worth checking out. I'll set up an interview with Ren Tanaka first."

"Thank you," Ogden said, relief softening his brow.

Will changed the subject and asked him questions about his NFL career. I kind of zoned out and enjoyed my salad while they reminisced about football.

When there was a lull in the conversation, I reached over and rested a hand on Will's thigh. He turned to me and I nodded. I'd made up my mind. Ogden was a good guy, with a good heart. I couldn't see him ridiculing me. "I'm ready," I whispered.

Will placed his hand on top of mine and held it there while he said, "Ogden, before we wrap up the subject of Hana, Darwin has something to tell you.

I'd like to ask that you keep an open mind." His tone deepened into a warning. "And keep in mind that she's trusting you with this information."

Ogden glanced from Will to me and then picked his napkin up off his lap. Wiping his mouth, his eyes grew guarded. "That sounds ominous."

How do I even begin? Guess it was like ripping off a Band-Aid, I just had to do it. "How do you feel about psychics?"

Ogden's mouth ticked up at the corner and his eyes softened. "Psychics? Well, I haven't thought much about 'em. But my mother was Jamaican and my father Scottish, so I grew up with an eclectic belief system. I'm pretty open-minded about it." He tilted his head. "You a psychic?"

"Not exactly. Like I can't tell people their future or anything like that." I took a deep breath and then just spit it out. "What I do is get visions from animals who've recently been traumatized."

"Wow," Ogden said. He glanced at Will for confirmation. Will nodded. "That's actually pretty cool."

I relaxed a little. Just a little though, because here was the personal part. "The reason I'm telling you this is because when I first met Daisy, I got a vision of Hana fighting with someone. Someone chucked a glass bowl at the wall. I assume it was you because of the shoe size... I only saw the feet."

Ogden's eyes widened. "Yeah. Yeah. That's... wow." He was shaking his head then he held up his hands. "Daisy didn't get hurt or anything."

"No, I know. She was just scared. But, can you tell us what that fight was about?"

His shoulders tensed up.

"Remember, we're just trying to prove Hana's innocence," Will said softly.

Ogden picked his napkin back up and busied himself folding it into a perfect square. When he was done, he placed it on his empty plate and not quite looking at me said, "Well, it wasn't actually a fight." He paused and finally made eye contact. "That's when I told Hana that Russo was going to be judging the Golden Lobster Contest." He swiped a big hand over his face. "Yeah, she blew up, started throwing things. I was yelling at her to calm down—that was wrong, but like I said, I don't handle stress well these days. Anyway, I was trying to get her to see that it wasn't worth her mental health to let this woman get to her. Hana was furious, though." He stopped and held out his hands. "I mean, not mad enough to kill Russo, she isn't that type of person. She broke down again that night. Got so depressed and just lost hope. Really scared me. Like I said, she'd only hurt herself."

Will's tone was gentle as he asked, "When was this?"

"The Saturday before last."

Will and I shared a look.

Yeah, more than enough time for Hana to come up with a plan and find the poisonous kind of pufferfish.

CHAPTER ELEVEN

Wednesday afternoon, a fast-moving, black storm rolled in over the Gulf. I leaned on the counter, watching sheets of rain flood the sidewalk in front of the boutique as thunder rumbled and shook the building. I sighed. As much as I enjoyed the rain, I hoped it would roll out just as quickly. Storms were not good for business.

Willow had stayed home with Daisy, so I didn't have to bring her to work with me today. She and Grandma Winters were working on the two pet birthday cakes due for delivery tomorrow. It was so nice having their help. I didn't feel like I was running around like a headless chicken so much anymore.

Mallory was sitting cross-legged on the wood floor brushing Goldie and fending off Petey as he tried to bite the brush and then the ends of her braids. "Stop it you little monster!" She laughed, nudging him away. Goldie wiggled on her back, forcing Mallory to brush her belly.

An umbrella pushed through the front door as a strobe of lightning lit up the sky. Will's face emerged from behind it, surprising me.

"Hey!" I rushed over. "Everything all right?"

He pressed a damp kiss on my lips, then held up a wet paper bag. "I was going to see if you wanted to have lunch in the park."

With a smile, I took the bag and peeked inside. "Well, this is a nice surprise. Sandwiches from Lonnie's. Yum."

He folded up the umbrella and leaned it against the door as I carried the bag to the table.

"Want some hot tea?" I asked.

"Sure." He waved to Mallory and then slid into a chair, rolling up the damp sleeves on his white dress shirt.

I poured hot water over two diffusers filled with chai oolong. Another crack of lightning flashed outside the window, a loud rumble of thunder right on its heels. "So, how'd your morning go?"

"Semi-productive. Skip Pascoe came in yesterday and gave us a writing sample. This morning our expert came back with their report. It's a match to the note left in Russo's car with all the dead fish, so he finally confessed to the threats."

"Really?" I unwrapped my sandwich. A warm, gouda grilled cheese. *Heaven on a rainy day.* "Does that mean y'all think he was the one who poisoned her?"

Will unwrapped his meatball sub with a shake of his head. "He had two of his kitchen workers with him there at the festival. They swear he was never alone and never went near the judging booth. So, unless they're both willing to put their necks on the line covering for their boss..." He didn't look convinced. "In any case, Pascoe's agreed to let us search his kitchen. Personally, I'm not liking him for the poisoning. I think he's all bark and no bite."

I frowned. "So, Hana's still your number one suspect?"

Hearing the disappointment in my voice, he reached over and squeezed my hand. "The tox report on the sample of pufferfish we found in Happi Sushi's kitchen should be back later this afternoon. We'll either charge her or release her at that point."

I watched a couple sharing an umbrella splash by outside the window. Then I turned back to Will. "Are you really going to talk to her sous-chef like you told Ogden you would?"

He finished swallowing a bite. "Yeah, I've got his home address. It's up by Sawgrass Park. Going to pay him a visit after lunch, in fact. And in a twist that may be coincidence or not, Pascoe told us he'd heard a rumor that Russo's final restaurant critique, which hasn't been printed yet, will be a review of Kam's."

I pulled a tiny piece of cheese from the bread and held it out for Goldie. She gently nibbled it off my fingers. "I guess that'd be easy to find out."

"Yep. Have a call in to the St. Pete journal. If it's true, we'll get a copy. See how bad it is. Could be motive."

"Hey, Sawgrass Park, that's out by the property Frankie found for the animal shelter. I can come with you and show it to you. We're so excited about it. Mallory can handle the boutique for an hour. Can't you, Mal?"

"Sure," Mallory said, pushing herself off the floor. "I've got nothing else going on in my life."

I rolled my eyes and whispered, "Bad date with that musician guy from the seafood festival."

Will glanced at Mallory with a sympathetic smile. "I guess that would be fine. If Tanaka has a pet, it'd be good to have you there." He winked at me and then his smile faded. He put down his sandwich. "Just so there are no secrets between us, I want you to know Cynthia's asked me to come over on Saturday. She needs help moving some boxes out of the garage that the previous tenants left there. One hour tops." He reached over and slipped his hand over mine. "You don't mind, do you?"

Mind? Oh, there were so many things going through my mind. Why *Will?* Why couldn't she hire someone to do that? But I knew why Will. I just wondered if he knew it. I unfroze my smile. "Of course not."

He didn't look convinced. *Why was I such a bad liar?* "You know there's nothing there between us anymore."

"Does she know that?" I bit my tongue. I didn't mean to let that slip out.

He squeezed my hand. "If she doesn't, she will. It'll give me the opportunity to clear up any misconceptions she has about that."

I shoved the cheese sandwich in my mouth to smother any more jealous thoughts that might pop out.

❖　❖　❖

We chucked our dripping umbrellas into the backseat, then Will pulled away from the future shelter property and merged onto I-275, headed toward Ren Tanaka's place.

"That's a great piece of property, already cleared and with water, sewer and electric hooked up. Hope they accept Frankie's offer. You said almost a full acre?" Will asked.

I tucked a strand of damp hair behind my ear. "Yep. And Frankie's found a great architectural firm with experience designing shelters. It's not as easy as throwing up four walls and some cages, you know. We have to think about noise control and air flow and pressure zones, sprinkler systems, drainage systems." My head was spinning. "Anyway, it's a lot. Luckily, Frankie knows everyone in this town. It really is going to be a huge team effort."

Will checked his side mirror and steered the sedan off the exit. "It's nice to see something good coming from Peter Vanek's senseless death. I'm sure he'd be proud."

"I sure hope so."

The rain had let up and only a light mist was falling as we knocked on Ren Tanaka's door.

It opened and a wiry, shirtless man glared at us. An orange tabby cat was tucked under one arm. "Yeah?"

The cat's yellow eyes regarded us with the same expression as its owner's, annoyed that we were interrupting their day.

Will motioned to the badge clipped to his belt. "Detective Blake. I'd like to ask you a few questions about Hana Ishida."

Ren Tanaka released the cat to the floor and swooped his arm in a mock gesture as the cat skittered away. We followed him deeper inside the small house. He held his hand out to the chrome and red leather bar stools. "Have a seat." Meanwhile, he strolled to the other side of the bar, into the kitchen.

I glanced around. Considering the plain stucco outside and the sandy, weed-filled yard, I wasn't expecting the inside of his house to be so posh. But it was. It had overstuffed, leather sofas, a crystal chandelier, large oil paintings in the living room area and a shiny, modern stainless-steel kitchen with a silver glass backsplash and copper range hood. It looked like he'd won one of those home-makeover shows.

Also, whatever he was cooking on the stove smelled delicious.

He grabbed a Hawaiian shirt off the counter and slipped his arms into it, though he didn't bother to button it up. "I have to watch this sauce, or it'll burn. What do you want to know?"

Will flipped his notepad open. "You work in Ms. Ishida's kitchen, as her sous-chef, correct?"

"Yep. Second in command of the kitchen. First to do the dirty work." He glanced back and smiled, but it didn't reach his raven-dark eyes. He returned his attention back to the sauce.

Will stared at the back of his head. "Were you at the seafood festival on Sunday?"

He shifted on his bare feet. "Nope. I wasn't needed. Hana wanted entire control of the dishes for the contest."

"Speaking of that. I heard that you may be the one who suggested she serve pufferfish as the main course?"

He glanced back at Will again and scoffed. "Well, yeah, but obviously not the toxic kind."

"Obviously," Will said with a friendly smile. "So, you didn't enter the festival at all? Not even to stop by the booth? See how things were going. Say hi."

Ren twisted a knob on the stove, then leaned against the counter and crossed his arms. "We don't have that kind of relationship, Detective. You can check with Marcus Block, the server who was helping her out in the booth. He'll verify I was never there."

Will had already interviewed Marcus to rule him out as a suspect, so he didn't write that down in his notebook. "Do you recall ever hearing Ms. Ishida threaten Ruth Russo?"

Ren shook his head, his black hair shining under the fluorescent lighting. "Nope, but it wasn't any secret she hated the woman... or why."

"So, you have no reason to believe the poisonous pufferfish Russo was served came from Ms. Ishida's kitchen?"

"I have no reason to believe that, no." He rubbed the back of his neck. "Look, Detective, there's a ban on harvesting pufferfish from the east coast, where they're toxic, so she couldn't have got the fish there. And there's only one importer that restaurants can get fugu from, that's Wako International. There are only seventeen restaurants in the US that are licensed to serve fugu, and Hana's restaurant isn't one of them, so she didn't get it from there, either. Other than that, even if she did want to poison Russo, I have no idea where she would've found toxic pufferfish."

Will wrote something in his notebook that I couldn't read. "Thanks. I'll confirm that."

The orange striped tabby hopped up on the bar, tail flicking. With a soft *meow*, it butted its head against the arm I was leaning my chin on.

Zap!

I flinched slightly as a wave of heat carried a vision through my body. A huge, gray muscular dog with cropped ears, heavy chain collar and blue eyes... its deep, clipped barking filled my head. I felt cornered.

"Excuse me." I moved quickly to the front door, pushed it open and began to do jumping jacks in the front yard until I felt the energy leave me with a loud pop in my ears. I walked in slow circles to calm my breathing.

The neighbor across the street was staring at me, clutching mail to her chest, her face unreadable. I waved. She hurried back inside her house. Shrugging, I took in a deep lungful of the rain-scented air and then headed back inside.

Will was writing something in his notebook. He glanced up at me, his eyes full of questions. I shook my head to let him know it wasn't anything important to the case. The cat had stretched out on the counter. Since it was safe now, I ran my hand from her ears and down her soft back to her tail. She chirped with pleasure, yellow eyes hooded.

"Is there a big gray dog around this neighborhood?" I asked.

Ren's eyes narrowed as he focused on me. "No. Why?"

I shrugged. "Just thought I saw one." Not a lie.

"One last thing I'd like to clear up, Mr. Tanaka." Will had that casual, relaxed posture he gets right before he asks the important question. "Previously you worked for Kam's Sushi Palace, correct?"

Ren turned his back and began to stir his sauce slowly. "That's right," he said without looking back.

"I hear they're Ms. Ishida's biggest rival. Why did you leave there and take the job at Happi Sushi?"

Ren knocked the wooden spoon on the edge of the pot a few times and then set it carefully on the counter. When he turned around, his eyes flashed with irritation. "Biggest rival? That's a laugh. Kam's is way out of Happi Sushi's league. That's like comparing a high scale steak house to McDonalds."

Will sat up straighter, his focus sharpening. "So, what you're saying is you chose to leave an upscale restaurant and go work at a fast food sushi place? Why?"

Ren folded his arms. "I didn't choose to leave. I got fired because of nepotism. Mr. Kam brought his nephew over from Nagoya and replaced me. I'm working at Happi Sushi to pay the bills until I can find something better. Guess I have to find another job faster if Hana goes down for murder, though."

Will scratched that down in his notebook. "All right. One more thing. Do you know anything about Ruth Russo's plan to review Kam's?"

Ren's nostrils flared. "Yeah, I heard a rumor she'd already been to Kam's. They won't know for sure until her review comes out. If they're even going to print it now that she's dead."

Will's expression stayed neutral, but his hand tensed around the pen. "You know Mr. Kam pretty well, I'm assuming?"

Ren uncrossed his arms and visibly forced himself to relax. "Sure."

"Do you think he'd have any reason to be worried about Russo's review being negative?"

Ren's eyes flicked toward the front door. "Nah. She reviewed Kam's a few years ago and gave it a decent review. Things have only improved. Of course, it is one person's opinion, and can hinge on something other than the food, like their mood or previous bias."

"One powerful person's opinion," Will stated. "One person who can make or break a restaurant with their words."

Ren shrugged casually, but his narrow jaw twitched. "Unfortunately."

Will dropped his business card on the counter. "Thanks for your time."

Will started the car and sat there, staring at Ren's house.

"Something bothering you?" I asked.

Will rubbed his jaw. "Yeah. I got the impression from everyone else that Happi Sushi's food was comparable to Kam's." He glanced at me. "Seems odd Tanaka would downplay that, considering that's where his paycheck is coming from, don't you think?"

I nodded. "He seemed pretty riled up at the thought of Kam's getting a bad review, too. Not the reaction I'd expect from someone who got fired from there."

Will's phone buzzed. "Detective Blake," he answered. "Yeah."

He listened to whoever was on the other end, his frown deepening the lines between his eyes. He stared at the car ceiling then blew out a deep breath. "Thanks for the update. I'll be back in about thirty minutes."

He hung up. A small growl of frustration escaped his throat as he backed out of the driveway. "The DNA results came back on the two pufferfish samples. Both are from the mid-Atlantic coast. Non-toxic."

"I'm sorry. I know you were hoping you had your man… or woman. So, this means you'll have to release Hana?"

"Yep." He turned onto the main road, his expression grim. "We don't have any hard evidence to hold her."

For a moment, I was relieved that Hana and Daisy would be reunited. But then an image of Hana's threat during the YouTube interview popped into my head. Was I being naïve thinking this woman wasn't capable of murder?

CHAPTER TWELVE

Mallory sat on the living room floor, trying to brush Daisy while we waited for Will to bring Hana over to pick her up. But Daisy was having none of it. She kept barking at the brush and then running in a circle around Mallory. She'd got Petey wound up, too, so he was trying to chase her, but kept getting in her way and getting knocked over. Goldie watched the show with a big, panting grin. In fact, they had us all grinning.

When the intercom buzzed, I opened the gate. But when the elevator door slid open, it wasn't Will who stepped out... it was Zach.

I rounded the kitchen counter and stood in front of him with my hands out. "This really isn't a good time."

He smirked, his dark eyes flashing as they roamed my face. "Good to see you, too."

I blushed and forced myself to stop noticing how good he smelled. "Sorry, I don't mean to be rude."

Goldie trotted up and sat in front of him, tail wagging for a pet. *Traitor.* As he bent over and stroked her head, he said, "I'll make it fast. I have some information on your father's whereabouts."

"Come in," Grandma Winters called from her perch on the sofa.

Zach shot me a bright smile and moved past me into the living room.

Rolling my eyes, I followed him.

As he lowered himself onto the loveseat, Lucky hissed, jumped off the back and padded up the stairs. I wished I was that immune to his charm.

"You found him?" Grandma Winters asked, her voice high with hope and a touch of surprise.

"I have. It's an old prison cave, one way in, one way out. You can guess what is guarding the entrance. So, there will be no sneaking around the sea-wolf. I'll have to engage. But that would mean Darwin has to take on Iris alone while I do."

They both glanced at me.

Grandma Winters shook her head slightly. "She's not ready."

I folded my arms self-consciously. "I've been practicing. I'm almost there."

Grandma Winters's expression shifted from concern to urgency. "If you can just get Ash free, he can help you get out."

Just then the intercom buzzed again. I groaned.

Zach watched me for a moment, and then he nodded with understanding. "I'll go."

When the elevator door opened, Will came face to face with Zach. He stepped out, his expression darkening. Hana was a small shadow behind him.

Wordlessly, Zach held up his palms and stepped around Will into the elevator. I was biting my thumb nail as Zach held my gaze until the elevator door slid closed.

"What the hell was he doing here?" Will whispered.

I opened my mouth and closed it. Then I glanced at Hana, who'd dropped to her knees and was happily letting Daisy plant slobbery kisses all over her face. "Not what you think. I'll explain later."

"I missed you, too," Hana cooed, pressing her forehead into Daisy's. Then she tilted her face up. Her skin was blotchy, her eyes red. "Thank you for taking such good care of her."

"She was no problem, really. You want a cup of tea or coffee?" I asked, trying to shake off the hot waves of jealousy coming from Will.

"I'd actually love some tea. Thank you."

"Great, have a seat in the living room." I went to the kitchen and put on the teapot. Half-listening to the burble of small talk coming from the living room, I thought about what Zach had found out. An old prison cave. One way in, one way out. So, he'll have to distract the sea-wolf while I slip in and find Father. I need to know how Iris has him bound, though, to be prepared. Is it a physical cage? The invisible one I felt before? It must be more than physical, or he'd be able to get himself out.

Carrying a tray into the living room, I let Hana, Grandma Winters and Willow take a cup. I noticed Daisy was laying across Hana's feet and smiled. "Guess she's making sure you don't go anywhere without her again."

"Thank you," Hana said, accepting the tea and glancing down at Daisy. "She usually goes everywhere with me. Even at the restaurant, she has a playroom set up in my office, so I'm sure she didn't understand why I'd left her." Then turned to Will. "Look, no hard feelings. I understand you were just doing your job. I'm the one who served pufferfish, and I understand all those angry interviews I did made me look guilty."

"I appreciate that," Will said, a hint of irony in his tone.

I cocked my head as I studied Will and realized he still wasn't convinced Hana was innocent. "Hana, you're sure no one had access to the food you served at the festival, besides Marcus Block."

She flicked her long hair off her shoulder. "I'm sure. Marcus didn't even touch it. I prepared the fish myself. I split one fish between the judges. All servings came from the same fish."

Her frustration wafted over me. If she was guilty, wouldn't she tell Will that someone else could've accessed the food?

Mallory had her legs stretched out in front of her on the floor, playing tug with Petey, but she was watching Hana curiously. "Do you have any theories on how only Ruth Russo ended up eating poisonous pufferfish?"

"I honestly don't," Hana said, staring into her teacup. "It makes no sense."

Willow shifted beside Hana, her tone thoughtful as she asked, "Will, how much pufferfish toxin would it take to kill a woman of Ruth Russo's size?"

"Not much. The doctor at the hospital said Russo weighed around 120 pounds, so it would've only taken 1 mg of TTX to be lethal."

Willow tapped her teacup with her index finger. "Could someone buy *just* the toxin?"

Will stroked Goldie's head as she leaned against his legs. Then he wrestled Gator out of her mouth and tossed it across the room. "Well, like I said before, you'd have to have a medical license."

"Some doctors own restaurants, don't they? As investments?" Willow asked. "Maybe it wasn't a restaurant owner but an investor who was upset with her."

"I suppose it's possible." Will gave Goldie one last pat as she returned, Gator held gently in her jaws, then pulled out his notebook. "We'd have to cross reference all the restaurants Russo gave bad reviews to with investors who have a medical license."

I sipped my tea as I dismissed that idea. I could tell Will was skeptical by his lack of enthusiasm, so I wouldn't waste my time on following that line of thinking. Then I remembered the photo I'd taken at the festival. "Oh, Will, I forgot to show you something." I got up and dug my phone out of my bag. Sitting back beside Will on the sofa, I pulled up the photo of the guy with the red hat. "I snapped a pic of this guy while Ruth Russo was being carried away on the gurney. He seemed a bit too happy about the situation."

Will enlarged the man's face. "I don't recognize him." Then he held out the phone to Hana. "Do you recognize this man by any chance?"

Hana leaned forward and accepted the phone. "Oh, sure. That's Phil Cunningham. He was my silent business partner when I owned Kabuto Grill." She handed Will back the phone. "He heard Russo was showing her face at the seafood festival and just stopped by to see the woman in person who'd lost him a quarter million dollars, but he doesn't have a medical license, and he's definitely not the murderer type."

Will handed me back my phone with a nod of approval. "Still, I'd like to have a word with him. Do you have his contact information?"

Hana set her teacup down and pulled her phone from a tiny, red purse. "Of course."

While Will jotted down his information, I said, "So, Oggie told us he wasn't fond of your sous-chef, Ren Tanaka."

Hana became very still as her eyes narrowed. "Really? Oggie said that? Wait, when did you speak to Oggie?"

"We had dinner with him." I decided to come clean since Oggie would probably tell her anyway. "Will needed to ask him about something I saw." I stumbled, this was the hard part. "I sort of... get images from animals who've suffered recent trauma. And when I touched Daisy, I saw a fight between you and Oggie. Someone threw a glass bowl and broke it."

"That's incredible." She shifted on the sofa, angling her body toward me. Daisy scratched at her leg and Hana hoisted her up onto her lap. "Yeah, I remember that day. I was furious with Oggie." She rested a hand on Daisy's back. "But, of course, he told you it was all a misunderstanding, right? Princess, his cat, was recently diagnosed with diabetes. Poor thing. I told him she was overweight, but he insists she's just 'fluffy.'"

Will and I exchanged a glance. *What was she talking about? Did Oggie lie to us about what the fight was about? Or was he just confused because of his memory issues?*

Will took the lead. "We'd like to hear your version of the event, if you don't mind."

She shrugged. "Well, he was over at my place. I went out to his car for my sunglasses I'd left in there and..." she paused, tilted her head and squinted at Will. "Did Oggie tell you he used to have a drug problem?"

"No, he didn't."

"I didn't think he would. He's really ashamed of it. Anyway, it was my fault, I jumped to conclusions and accused him of using again. He's not."

"Glad to hear that," I said. Oggie seemed like a nice guy, and I'd seen enough nice guys get their lives ruined by drugs. But I still didn't understand what this had to do with his cat.

Will was trying to figure out the connection, too. "So, the fight was about the fact you thought he was using drugs again? Because of something you found in his car?"

"Yes. Princess's insulin needles."

"Ah," Will said.

Well, I guess that explains why he lied about what the fight was about. He was probably ashamed of his previous drug use.

Will rubbed his forehead. The shadows were deepening beneath his eyes. "Oggie didn't just say he didn't like Ren Tanaka, he said he didn't trust him. Thought it was plausible Kam sent Tanaka to work for you, to sabotage your restaurant somehow. Framing you for Russo's murder would do the trick. He's worked for you for how long now?"

"Just two months." Hana's face paled. Her hand fluttered to her throat. "You think they would go to all that trouble to frame me for murder?"

Daisy must have sensed her owner's distress. She stretched higher up her chest and rested her head on Hana's shoulder.

Will held up a hand. "We're just exploring theories right now. But that interview, where you suggested giving Russo a special fugu dish, could've given someone the idea. The only inconsistency here is Tanaka said your restaurant wasn't a threat to Kam's. That it was like comparing McDonalds to a steak house."

We all watched her reaction and it wasn't good.

Her face was frozen in an expression of horror. "McDonalds? McDonalds?" She shook her head vehemently. "No. That's not true. My restaurant is every bit as good as Kam's, and I know for a fact he was losing business to me. My customers tell me all the time they used to go to Kam's but now come to Happy Sushi." Her anger simmered down as she thought of something. "Also, at the festival, Phil told me he'd just got his hands on Kam's annual audit report, and his top line revenue was down. He thought it'd make me feel better. Plus Mr. Kam just laid off twenty percent of his staff two months ago." The anger broke like a dam. "So, why would Ren say that?" Tears were spilling out onto her cheeks now. Daisy was trying to lick them off.

Willow handed her a tissue.

"I don't know," Will said. "But we've also heard that Russo may have reviewed Kam's before she died. Maybe Mr. Kam thought killing her would mean she wouldn't have time to write the review, or the review wouldn't be published. Bonus that he could implicate you and ruin your business at the same time. Either way, a conversation with Mr. Kam is in order. If it's true that you were affecting his business, Oggie's theory might not be so far-fetched. I've heard the restaurant business is pretty cut-throat."

Her hand shook as she rubbed her temple. "You have no idea."

CHAPTER THIRTEEN

"Good morning, Darwin." Gillian Smith waved as she entered the boutique Thursday morning. Her black and white Great Dane, Monty, lumbered in beside her. "I had a call that the ramp we ordered was in?"

"Yes, Ma'am." I came around the counter. "I'll go grab that for ya. Hey, Monty." I slid my hands under the big dog's chin and rubbed. He panted with squinting, happy eyes and a string of drool dropped onto my arm.

I laughed. "You sure do make me miss Karma." It'd been a little over a year since I'd seen the mastiff.

I'd befriended Karma, along with his owner, Mad Dog, when I'd first moved to St. Pete. Karma was also the first animal who'd got me involved in solving a murder because of my visions. Nina, the mastiff's new dog-mom and Mad Dog's ex-wife, was nice enough to text me pictures of the Karma occasionally. They almost always included Mad Dog's daughter, Mariah, because apparently those two were inseparable. Hopefully they'd all come for a visit soon.

I patted Monty's head with a sigh. "Be right back."

"You need help with that?" Charlie called from the grooming room when she saw me wrestling the large box from storage.

"Thanks, I think I got it," I called back. Dragging it out front, I laid it down flat and put my hands on my hips. "Maybe the two of us can get it to your truck."

Gillian was spinning the countertop display of Swarovski Crystal keychains. "That's okay, my husband should be here any second. He was just trying to find a close parking space." She plucked a keychain from its hook. "This kind of looks like a Great Dane." She examined the crystal dog above the words 'Dog Mom,' then placed it on the counter. "I'll take it."

Her husband came in as I was ringing up her purchases. Monty rose and greeted him with a tail wag that knocked over our grooming sign. "Sorry," he said sheepishly. "Sit, Monty."

I handed Gillian her bag, then pulled a peanut butter treat from the jar for Monty. He launched himself forward and rested his jowls on the counter. I grinned as I gave him the cookie, then reached for a towel to wipe the drool off the glass. "Good luck training him to use the ramp."

"Thanks. He's such a chicken when it comes to new things, so we'll need that luck," Gillian said.

⁂

Will picked me up for lunch, but we were going to make a stop at Mr. Kam's place first. In the car, he slid a piece of fax paper out of a leather binder.

"The rumor was true. Russo wrote a review of Kam's Sushi Palace and it's pretty ugly."

I quickly scanned the fax and cringed. "The fried sushi rolls were soggy and tasted like old oil. Wow, she really didn't hold back."

"I know. Sounds like she was in a particularly bad mood that day. Let's go see how Mr. Kam reacts."

We pulled around the circle drive and parked in front of the large Spanish Mediterranean-style home. Will's knock triggered a flurry of deep barking.

I was startled to see the large, gray pit bull I'd seen in my vision appear behind the glass door. His cropped ears and tail stood erect. His blue eyes were locked on us, a deep growl reverberating in his barrel chest. I reflexively stepped behind Will.

A stocky, bald man with a goatee and wearing black slacks and a white, button-down shirt approached. His command sent the dog away from the door as he opened it.

"Mr. Kam?" Will asked. The man gave a curt nod. "I'm Detective Blake. This is Darwin Winters."

Will had set up the interview with Mr. Kam here at his home, where it was quieter, instead of at the restaurant, so he was expecting us. Still, he didn't seem all that thrilled as he moved aside and waved us in.

I hesitated when I noticed the dog sitting a few feet away, jaw clenched tight, his attention still locked on us.

"Don't worry about Rocky. He only attacks on command." Turning when he realized we weren't following him, Mr. Kam smiled. "Just a joke. He wouldn't hurt a fly. Come on." He led us through the house. Rocky followed close behind.

We filed into the living room, which was decorated with an oriental rug, a mirrored wall, a life-size gold Buddha statue in the corner and enough plants to give the impression of stepping into a jungle. We took a seat on the rust-colored leather sofa. Mr. Kam settled into the matching armchair across from us. Rocky plopped down at his owner's feet, but he was still keeping an eye on us.

He was definitely the dog in the vision I'd got from Ren's cat. If the two men were close enough that Mr. Kam was hanging out at Ren's house, why would Mr. Kam fire Ren? Or did Mr. Kam just visit Ren that one time with Rocky in tow?

"I assume this is about Ruth Russo's death?" Mr. Kam smiled easily.

"What have you heard about it?" Will asked.

He lifted his hands slightly from the arms of the chair. "Just that she was poisoned with pufferfish at the seafood festival. Which was served by Hana Ishida."

Will's tone was friendly. "Do you think Ms. Ishida is capable of killing Ms. Russo?"

Mr. Kam stared at the floor, deep in thought for a moment. "I don't know Ms. Ishida personally. But I've seen the interviews she gave after Kabuto Grill closed down, including the one where she threatened to serve Russo fugu. So..." he shrugged.

Interesting that he admitted seeing that interview. If he'd gotten the idea to poison Ruth Russo with the pufferfish—and frame Hana—from that interview, would he admit seeing it so readily?

Will made a note of that. "The thing is, we tested the pufferfish Ms. Ishida served the judges and a sample from Happi Sushi's kitchen, and they were both the non-toxic kind."

Mr. Kam shifted in the chair, pulling the collar of his shirt away from his neck. "Honestly, that makes sense. She's not licensed to buy fugu anyway. I'm not sure where she'd get it."

"Any restaurants in the area you know of that are licensed?"

"Yes. Mine." He stared at Will defiantly.

I glanced at Will. His jaw twitched. I don't think he was expecting that answer.

"And when was the last time you purchased fugu?"

"About four years ago as a special request. It's not a very popular dish in the states. You can verify that with Wako International in New York. They're the only company the FDA's approved to import fugu, because they import from processing facilities licensed by the Japanese government."

Will jotted that in his notebook. "Mr. Kam, is it true that you've cut your staff by twenty percent in the last few months?"

Mr. Kam was silent, but his face reddened. After a few tense moments he gave a curt nod. "The restaurant business is not an easy one to keep afloat."

"Do you attribute the hard times to losing business to Happi Sushi?"

Mr. Kam tried to chuckle, but it sounded forced. "I'm not worried about Happi Sushi. People always flock to the shiny new thing, but they eventually come back to the best service and food."

The questions were coming faster now. "Why did you fire Ren Tanaka? I hear he's a talented sous-chef. It has to bother you that he's now working for your competition."

"Ren is very talented. But my nephew is in the states now, and he's also very talented. I had to choose family."

"So, no hard feelings between you and Mr. Tanaka?" Will asked.

"I haven't spoke to him since he left, but I hope not."

Now I really needed to find out when Rocky was at Ren's house. If it was in the last two months, Mr. Kam was covering something up.

"Were you aware that Ms. Russo had been in your restaurant recently?"

Mr. Kam's hand tensed into a fist. "I had suspected as much but wasn't completely sure. As you're no doubt aware, no one knew what she looked like. But this woman, she came in alone before the dinner rush, ordered a lot of food and spent a lot of time tapping away on her phone. I thought about sending over a glass of Russo's favorite wine, to see how she reacted but decided it'd be best if she didn't think we suspected her."

Will leaned forward. "You didn't know what she looked like but knew her favorite wine?"

His fingers tapped the chair arms. "A few years ago, it was the thing that almost outed her. She stopped ordering it after that."

Will and I shared a look. Then Will slipped the fax paper out of his leather binder and handed it to Mr. Kam. "Here's an advanced copy of her review."

We watched as Mr. Kam's face remained calm, but his eyes were blazing when he looked up. "Will this still be published? Even though she's… no longer working there."

"That's what I'm told. So, you were worried about a bad review coming?"

He leaned his elbows on his knees, head hanging. "I was hoping not, but the day I suspected it was Russo in my dining room, my staff managed to do everything wrong."

As Will circled back, asking the same questions in a different way, Rocky pushed himself up and stretched his back legs. Giving himself a good shake, he ambled around the coffee table. I kept still as his cold, wet nose sniffed first my foot, then moved up my bare leg. All the smells from the pet boutique must be like a smorgasbord to him. When he reached my elbow, he nudged it and shoved his large, blocky head beneath my arm.

Zap!

A long, loud rumble of thunder filled my head. Bright, white light flashed outside a screen door. My body was trembling.

The energy zinged through my body and out my free arm as I shook it vigorously. Not a bad one. Curious, though. The view of the screen door looked an awful lot like Ren's place. Definitely wasn't this house.

I stroked the side of Rocky's velvety head as he rested it in my lap, amused by the fact that this huge dog was afraid of storms. Poor thing. He stayed there until Will signaled that we were done.

"Looks like someone made a friend," Mr. Kam said as he led us to the door.

"He really is a big baby, isn't he?" I gave Rocky one last scratch under his chin. "You know sometimes this breed can have storm phobias. Be afraid of thunder."

Mr. Kam shoved his hands in his slacks pockets and nodded vigorously. "I think he does actually. He hides in the shower even before we can hear the thunder."

I glanced down at Rocky, who had his eyes lifted to meet mine. I rubbed a cropped ear between my fingers. "I co-own Darwin's Pet Boutique on Beach Drive. If you come in, I can give you some flower essence to help calm him during storms. It's all-natural ingredients." *With just a touch of magick.*

"Flower essence, huh?" He raised a brow. "Sure, why not."

Once we got in the car, Will didn't waste any time calling Wako International and verifying that Kam's hadn't received an order of fugu for four years. "So, no one else in the state of Florida has ordered fugu from you in that time?" He rubbed his forehead. "Okay, thank you."

"So, he was tellin' the truth?" I asked as we pulled away.

"About that, yes." He tapped his fingers on the steering wheel. "Why do you think Ren Tanaka failed to mention his former employer was licensed to serve fugu?"

"I don't know. Seems like he'd know that would be important to share. Maybe he was protecting Mr. Kam?"

"Maybe. Then again, I didn't ask. And he seems to be the kind of person who won't share unless asked outright."

"But is it really relevant? I mean, I guess Mr. Kam could've kept it frozen that long, but he didn't even know Hana four years ago, so he definitely wasn't plotting against her back then."

Will nodded. "All right. I think it's time to look at other ways Russo ingested TTX besides in the actual pufferfish."

"So, we're looking for someone with a medical license."

Will glanced over at me, one corner of his mouth pushing up. "Yes, I guess *we* are."

I grinned, angling in my seat to face him. "Why, Detective, are you finally admitting I'm a valuable asset to this investigation?"

A deep chuckle filled the car. "I plead the fifth, Miss Winters."

"Mhm. I'll take that as a yes."

He reached over and intertwined our fingers. His thumb rubbed the purple square stone on my ring finger. He suddenly glanced over at me with a more serious expression. "We do make a good team." Then, clearing his throat, he said, "I couldn't help but notice your reaction when Rocky put his head on your lap. Anything important there?"

"Just some slight trauma from a recent storm. Although, the image was of a screen door, not the glass door at Mr. Kam's house. I can't be sure, but it looked an awful lot like Ren's place."

Will squeezed my hand with a sigh. "Unfortunately, lots of screen doors in Florida."

As Will drove and got lost in his own thoughts, I was feeling pretty good about things. It was getting easier for Will to ask me about my visions. It didn't seem like the elephant in the room anymore. But then I remembered he hadn't pushed me to explain what Zach was doing in my house. I sighed.

There was the daggone hulking elephant.

CHAPTER FOURTEEN

Frankie had called to let me know that they'd accepted our offer on the shelter property. We were both over the moon. While we waited on the permits, she wanted to get the ball rolling. So, after we closed up the boutique, I drove her out to the property to meet with the general contractor and sign some paperwork.

While Frankie and the contractor discussed the architect's schematic drawings over the hood of my VW Beetle, I let Goldie out of the car. We walked the edges of the property, me trying to picture the finished shelter, Goldie snuffling in the dirt, enjoying the new smells.

I shielded my eyes with my hand and looked up at the shifting mountains of clouds. "I hope you can see your dream materializing from wherever you are, Peter."

One of the clouds in particular caught my eye. It was drifting into the shape of a dog. I smiled. "I'll take that as a sign that you can."

Speaking of dogs, I really needed to find out when Rocky was at Ren Tanaka's house. That had been gnawing at me since we'd left Mr. Kam's place.

When I saw Frankie shake the contractor's hand and roll up the drawings, I made my way back to the car, Goldie trotting in front of me.

"We're really doing this." Frankie's face was shiny with sweat and joy.

I grinned back at her. "We sure are." I opened the car door and let Goldie jump in the back seat, then clipped the seat belt tether to her harness. "Hey, do you mind if we make a quick stop before heading home?"

"'Course not."

I drove back to Ren's house, since it was nearby, but pulled into the driveway of the house across the street from him. "Be right back."

The neighbor's front window blinds moved, then the door opened before I could knock.

"Yes?" the woman clutching the top of her worn robe asked.

"Hi, Sorry to be a bother, ma'am. I just have a quick question. Do you recall seeing a large, gray pit bull at the house across the street?"

Her thin brows raised under pink hair curlers. "You mean Rocky? Yeah, he comes around a bunch with his owner." She glanced around me, her voice rising with interest. "Did he maul someone?"

"No. Nothing like that."

Her posture collapsed with disappointment.

I crossed my fingers, hoping she was as nosey as I thought she was. "When was the last time you saw Rocky there?"

"On Sunday."

"This past Sunday? Like four days ago?" I asked. It did storm then. When she gave a curt nod, I thanked her for her time and headed back to the car.

Goldie sniffed my hair and licked my arm as I slid back into the driver's seat. I stroked under her chin, giving Ren's house one last glance. He'd lied to Will about his relationship with Mr. Kam, too. *Why?*

"Was that about Russo's murder?" Frankie asked, cleaning her large, black sunglasses with the tail of her shirt.

"It was." As I backed my car out of the driveway, I pointed my chin at Ren's house across the street. "Hana's sous-chef, Ren Tanaka, lives there. He used to work for Kam's Sushi Palace. When Will interviewed Ren, he seemed really upset Kam's might get a bad review from Ruth Russo. We couldn't figure out why he was being so protective of someone who'd fired him." I braked as a squirrel darted into the middle of the street. "Plus Mr. Kam said he hadn't seen Ren since he'd fired him two months ago. Which was a lie. The neighbor just told me she saw him here four days ago with his dog."

She slipped her glasses back on. "What does all that mean?"

I tapped the steering wheel with my thumbs. "Not sure. Possibly that Mr. Kam and Ren Tanaka were in cahoots to take down Hana's restaurant. And possibly poisoning Ruth Russo and framing Hana was part of that plan. Only, we can't figure out where the poison came from, if it didn't come from an actual pufferfish."

Frankie pulled sunscreen from her purse. "The toxin works immediately right?"

"Yep."

She rubbed the white lotion onto her pale, freckled arms. "Then it could've been in something else she ate or drank around that time."

I stopped at the stop sign a little more suddenly than I meant to. I stared at Frankie, but I wasn't seeing her. I was seeing Ruth Russo's Tweet about the wine an anonymous person had given her. "Something she drank! Heavens on a hilltop, Frankie. You're a genius."

I dug my phone out of the bag behind my seat. Goldie took the opportunity to give me a lick on the cheek. I had to leave a message. "Will, it's me. You need to test the Chateau Ste.Veuve wine bottle. And check Ruth Russo's Twitter account. She'd posted something about someone giving her a bottle of her favorite wine at the seafood festival. The poison could've been in there." I held a palm to my forehead as I tried to pull together the threads we had so far. "Didn't Mr. Kam mention he knew what Ruth Russo's favorite wine was? Also, Mr. Kam lied about not talking to Ren since he left. The neighbor said she saw him and Rocky at Ren's place on Sunday. Call me." I hung up, my adrenaline pumping. Clues were finally pointing to someone besides Hana.

"Sounds like maybe Hana's off the hook," Frankie said, tossing the sunscreen back in her bag. "That's good news for Daisy. Lord knows we don't need another homeless dog in the world." As I nodded in agreement, Frankie added, "Speaking of homeless dogs. Mallory mentioned you're still thinking about adopting Sandy?"

I sighed. Sandy was an older golden retriever mix I'd met at the shelter a few weeks ago while we were investigating Peter Vanek's murder. "Yeah, I actually took Goldie there to see if they got along, and you should've seen the two of them. Thick as thieves immediately, sniffing and chasin' each other around that small room. She's just the sweetest girl. Breaks my heart to think of her sleeping in that cage every night without a family to love." A lump formed in my throat. "I'd take her in a heartbeat if I thought I had the time to take care of her properly. It's just I've got Goldie and Petey at the pet boutique with me all day as it is. And Sandy's diabetic, so she needs shots three times a day. That's a lot of responsibility." I groaned. "How do you know when you're taking on too much?"

"Usually I don't know until something gives." She patted my knee. "Don't worry, sugar. It'll work out the way it's supposed to."

That night, even though I was exhausted, I stayed up late practicing my water magick. I had to be ready for when Grandma Winters said it was time to rescue Father. Bringing my energy into resonance with water had become like breathing. I didn't even have to think about it. But there was a final barrier, a final, critical step I hadn't reached yet: tapping into the original, Universal Consciousness. That unlimited source of power Grandma Winters had told us about.

I opened my eyes and stared at the water in the bowl as it settled down. "But how do I get there?"

A soft rap on the door interrupted my thoughts. "Come in." I could hear the edge of frustration in my own voice.

Grandma Winter's white silk robe fluttered as she stepped in and looked me over. Her eyes glowed in the dim light and energy radiated from her in intense waves. Nodding, she opened the door wider. "It's time, girls."

My sisters entered the room, looking both tentative and excited.

"What's going on?" I asked as Willow lowered herself to sit on my left, Mallory doing the same on my right.

Willow rested a warm hand on my back and offered me a reassuring smile. "We're here to help."

Grandma Winters sank onto the zafu cushion across from us and folded her hands. "While it's true that each of you embodies an energy signature that is in resonance with one aspect of nature, there is a force greater than this elemental magick. A force that is at the very fabric of life itself. I've talked to you girls about tapping into this Universal Consciousness for creative power. Now we're going to practice getting there by tuning into Love, which is the same frequency. And I don't mean love as in the chemical cascade of emotions, I mean the unconditional Love that is the bond you share. The same bond that holds all experience together. Join hands now."

My sisters silently slid their hands into mine, sending energy like warm water flowing up my arms.

My eyes fell shut as Grandma Winters began to talk us through the first exercise.

CHAPTER FIFTEEN

"Hey, Darwin, come check out Goldie." Mallory's laughter reached me from the back of the boutique.

Closing the top of the glass case after refilling the rows of homemade treats, I checked the time. Ten minutes until opening. Anxiety churned my stomach. Today was going to be Charlie's first time taking pet portraits at the boutique, so it was going to be a busy day. The best I could hope for was controlled chaos.

I rounded the end of the aisle where Charlie had set up a cloth backdrop, a portable softbox and her camera on a tripod. Goldie was sitting with a bright pink feather boa wrapped around her neck. Her mouth was stretched in a panting grin.

I crossed my arms and chuckled. "Looks like you have the perfect model there."

Goldie lifted a paw. There was a click and burst of flash as Charlie captured the pose. "What a natural."

"What a ham," Mallory said. She put Petey down, which turned out to be a mistake.

Petey pounced onto the end of the feather boa. Yanking back with little puppy growls, he managed to slip it from Goldie's neck. She happily grabbed a mouthful of feathers and joined in the game of tug.

"Oops, sorry. Should've seen that coming." Mallory scooped Petey back up and got him to release the boa. She pulled a few pink feathers from his mouth. "Not in your diet, little man."

I retrieved the damp boa from Goldie and draped it across the box of hats, bowties and other cute accessories. "Can we help with anything else?"

Charlie grinned and rubbed her hands together. "Nope. I think I'm ready."

I turned to Mallory. "The appointments are booked every fifteen minutes, with a forty-five-minute break for lunch. Your job is going to be to keep things moving as quickly and smoothly as humanly possible."

Her green eyes twinkled. "*Humanly* possible?"

I shot her a disapproving look.

She rolled her eyes and patted her thigh with her free hand. "Come on, Goldie. One last trip outside before the craziness begins."

And craziness it was. The first two appointments were waiting outside the door when we opened. After that, the boutique filled with a steady flow of pets and their owners. Luckily, everyone seemed to be having a good time. Since it was a lot of locals, the women ended up hanging around for a bit after their pet portraits were taken, which meant they also shopped while chatting.

I handed Jeanie her receipt. "Here you go. Snookie's portrait will be ready for pickup next Friday."

Will came through the door and navigated his way around the crowd. He waved when he found an open spot to stand in front of our pet adoption bulletin board.

I held up my index finger and mouthed, "One sec."

Jeanie lifted her mini Schnauzer's paw and waved it at me. "We'll see you Friday then."

I slipped around the counter and over to Will. He held up a brown bag. "I brought lunch, but it doesn't look like a good time."

"Pet portrait day." I glanced at the clock and pressed a hand to my gurgling stomach. "But, we're about to take a forty-five-minute break for lunch so perfect timing." I glanced around. "Though I still have to man the register. Can I wolf down whatever's in that bag in fifteen minutes?"

His mouth curved into that sexy smirk I loved so much. "You can sure try."

We sat at the tea table. I tilted my face to the bright sunlight streaming through the window. It was the first moment I had to appreciate the gorgeous summer day and I soaked it in. Goldie bumped my feet as she snuck under the table. Guess she needed a break from all the excitement, too.

"So, any news?" My mouth watered as I unwrapped the fat, veggie stuffed hummus wrap.

Will pulled napkins from the bag. "Yes, in fact."

"Yeah?" I leaned forward, making sure I could hear him over the conversations going on in the boutique.

"After re-evaluating Russo's Twitter account, I went back through the evidence collected from the festival and found the Chateau Ste. Veuve wine bottle. It had rolled quite a distance so while it was collected, it wasn't tested yet. Also, found the note that said, 'for all you do.' Now that we know they have significance, we're expediting the processing of both items for traces of TTX and prints."

I washed down a bite of hummus wrap with a swig of tea. "That's great news. If the killer didn't use gloves, you should be able to get prints off the bottle easily enough. Is it possible to get prints from the note, too?"

Will picked up his sandwich. "Sure. They use a chemical that causes the oils from fingerprints imbedded in the paper to fluoresce a bright purple." He flashed me a smile. "Like the color of your eyes."

I leaned over the table and planted a kiss on his lips. Then, checking to make sure no one was waiting to check out at the register, I asked, "Anything else?"

Will took a swig of his water, his blue eyes glittering playfully. "You're also kind of cute when you're hungry."

My mouth twisted in a grin. "I meant anything else about the case, smarty pants."

He looked pleased with himself. "Well, our guys checked all the restaurant owners and investors who Russo had given bad reviews to over the last five years. They didn't come up with a single person with a medical license, so that's a dead end. But I'm heading up to Tampa after this to interview Phil Cunningham, Hana's previous business partner. He doesn't have a medical license, either, but he was at the festival, so he has both motive and opportunity. And of course, I'll have to re-interview Tanaka and Kam, since they both lied. I'll bring 'em into the station. Make it more official."

"Something is going on with those two for sure." I took another bite, chewing thoughtfully. "Why hide the fact that they're still in contact?" I glanced over as Sarah Applebaum approached the counter with her Shih Tzu, Lady Elizabeth, and a basketful of items. "Shoot. Gotta go ring her up." I needed to invite her to the charity event Frankie'd set up at Fresco's Waterfront Bistro, too. Wrapping up the rest of my sandwich, I scooted out of the chair and snuck another kiss. "Thanks for lunch and good luck in Tampa. Call me later?"

"How about a late dinner tonight?"

"If I'm still on my feet at the end of this day, you've got yourself a date."

⚜ ⚜ ⚜

I was cleaning up a bag of cat litter that had busted open on the floor when a dark-haired teenage girl shyly approached me. "Excuse me?"

I leaned on the broom, grateful for the break. "Yes?"

She eyed the mess at my feet and hesitated. "Sorry to bother you, but my father sent me to get something for our dog, Rocky. He said you told him you could help with his storm phobia?"

I straightened up, adrenalin giving me a much-needed energy boost. "Oh, yes, of course. Give me one sec." As I made my way back to the storage room, my mind was racing. This was Mr. Kam's daughter. Surely she'd know the real story about her father's relationship with Ren Tanaka. I needed to bring it up, but very carefully so I didn't make her suspicious. If she told her father I was asking questions, that might give him a head's up before Will could question him again.

I carried the aspen and rock rose flower essence back to the register, biting the inside of my cheek.

Think, Darwin.

"You can add five or so drops to his water or put them under his tongue if he'll let you."

She nodded with a ghost of a smile. "In his water bowl it goes."

I took my time wrapping up the glass bottle in tissue paper. "So, do you work in your father's restaurant?"

She eyed me warily. "I help out where I'm needed."

There was an awkward silence. I wondered if Mr. Kam had warned her not to discuss his business with me while she was here. I tried to lighten the mood with humor. "Let me guess, dish duty?"

"Yes," she said with a soft chuckle. "But I start college in the fall, so no more kitchen duty." She glanced down at the tiny diamond on her ring finger, moving it around thoughtfully.

"Pretty ring," I said. "When's the wedding?"

"Oh." She blushed. "It's not an engagement ring. More like a promise ring. We're not ready for marriage, but my boyfriend, Ren, is afraid I'll forget him when I go away to college."

My heart picked up speed, but I managed to keep my tone neutral. "Ren Tanaka?"

"Yes." She glanced up at me. Her large, kohl-lined eyes registered surprise. "You know him?"

I reached under the counter for a bag. "Your father told us Ren used to work for him, before he hired family to take his place."

Her skin flushed. "Yeah, that was wrong and made no sense. Ren is the best sous-chef around. I don't understand why Dad let him go for Kobe, who can't even chop an onion without cutting himself." She pulled her knobby shoulders back and flared her nostrils with that same teenage defiance I recognized from Mallory. "Anyway, it's a sore subject between us."

"Family's are tough," I offered, handing her a bag with the flower essence. "I imagine Ren is hoppin' mad at your father, too?"

"Thanks," she said, taking the bag. "Actually, no. Ren's being weirdly understanding about the whole thing. He and Dad still play golf all the time."

Bingo! Confirmation of their ongoing relationship straight from Mr. Kam's daughter. "Well, good for him for not holding a grudge. Sounds like you got yourself a good guy there."

Her expression softened. "Yeah, I guess you're right. I should be grateful Ren is so forgiving. Thanks."

I watched her leave and crossed my arms. I couldn't wait to tell Will I'd got confirmation of Ren and Mr. Kam's buddy-buddy relationship. I'd have to wait though, because the boutique was still hopping.

When we finally locked the doors and turned around the 'Closed' sign, the ache in my feet I'd been ignoring all day hit me. I toed off my sandals and collapsed into a chair.

"I'd say that was a success!" Charlie said. Her eyeliner was smeared under her eyes and her pink hair was damp around her face, but she was beaming. "I don't think I've ever had so much fun."

"Maybe you're missing your calling as a photographer," I said, rubbing the ball of my foot.

She stopped and thought about that. "Nah. My dad always told me if I found something I loved, just keep it as a hobby."

"Probably good advice. Anyway, great job today."

Mallory walked up from the back. She still had a bounce in her step.

I leaned an elbow on the table, trying to gather enough energy to finish closing up. "Hey, Mal, if you do the floors, I'll do the register."

"Sure. I'm gonna run the dogs across the street first. Be back." She scooped an antsy Petey out of his pen and grabbed Goldie's leash. Goldie trotted past her, beating her to the door.

"Hey, Mal?" I called.

She twisted the lock on the door then glanced over at me. "Yeah?"

"What do you think about me adopting Sandy? Would I be taking on too much?"

She adjusted the little ball of fur squirming in the crook of her arm and smirked. "Yes." She pushed open the door and then added, "unless I stayed around to help out."

I watched the door swing closed behind her. *Did that mean she was thinking about it? Would she stay even if Willow went back to Savannah to keep*

Mom company? I knew I couldn't push her. I'd just have to wait and see.

While I was forcing my tired brain to concentrate on counting the change, the door cracked open and a deep voice called. "Hello?"

My heart somersaulted as I clutched my chest.

Oggie pushed the door open with his knee, a big grin on his face.

"Lord have mercy, Oggie, you scared the bejeezus out of me." I grinned back. "Come in, come in. Whatcha got there?"

Oggie's arms were loaded down with brown paper bags. "Hana sent me by. She made y'all dinner as a way of saying thanks for taking care of Daisy."

"Really? Aw, she didn't have to do that." I peered into the bags as he unloaded them onto the table. Delicious, spicy scents drifted from them. "Mmmm. That smells like heaven." I glanced up with a smirk. "There's enough food in here to feed an army."

He chuckled. "Hana doesn't know how to do anything halfway."

"Well tell her thank you for us." I studied his face. "You seem in better spirits than when I saw you last."

His large hand rubbed the back of his neck sheepishly. "Yeah. If Hana's happy, I'm happy. It's as simple as that."

"Hana's a lucky girl. So, things are going good at Happi Sushi? I was kind of worried folks would avoid eating at a place where the owner was suspected of poisoning someone."

"You'd think." He shook his head. "But, seems like their curiosity has won out. She's packed tonight."

"Huh. Guess you never can tell."

"Well, I gotta get back. I'll pass on your gratitude."

"Thanks, Oggie. And tell Hana to bring Daisy in for a visit sometime soon."

"Will do."

Mallory was bringing the dogs back in as Oggie was leaving. "Who was that?"

"Hana's boyfriend." I grabbed my phone. "He brought us dinner she made as a thank you for taking care of Daisy."

It only rang twice before Will picked up. "Hey."

"Hey, yourself. Just come over when you're done. No need to go out for dinner. Oggie brought over some food Hana made for us. And when I say 'some' I mean enough to feed an army."

There was silence.

"Will?"

"I'm here. It's just... do you think it's a good idea to eat food Hana made?"

I rolled my eyes. "I don't think she's a killer, Will. Besides, it smells like it'll be worth the risk."

Will chuckled. "Can't argue with that logic. All right, I'll see you at your place in about an hour."

CHAPTER SIXTEEN

When Will stepped out of the elevator, he looked beat. His jaw had a slight five o'clock shadow and he'd removed his tie and untucked his shirt. After he gave Goldie and Petey some ear rubs, I pressed my face against his chest and listened to his heartbeat. He dropped his cheek to rest on the top of my head. Being in his arms felt like coming home.

"Rough day?" I asked.

"Better now," he whispered, then pressed his lips against my still-damp-from-the-shower hair. "You smell like flowers."

I smiled, feeling woozy from being so happy in the moment.

"You two lovebirds wanna take a seat. We're starving," Mallory said, as she passed us, carrying plates of soba noodles and sushi from the kitchen.

I stuck my tongue out at her as I led Will to the table.

Willow brought more dishes behind her, stopping and almost toppling forward as she tried to avoid stepping on Petey. "Petey, for heaven's sake."

"I got him," Mallory said, scooping him up and depositing him on the sofa. "Stay."

To our surprise, he laid down and obeyed.

"Hey, good job, Mal," I said as she slid into the seat beside Grandma Winters. "I'm impressed."

"Discipline is important," Grandma Winters said, her eyes gleaming at Mallory. "And what else is important?"

"Attention and intention," we three girls said in unison. We shared a look and broke out in laughter. After the night of practicing our magick together, our bond felt stronger than it had in years.

Grandma Winters winked at Will. "They *can* be taught."

I narrowed my eyes at Grandma Winters. She really seemed to like Will, despite knowing about his skepticism when it came to all things magick.

Will shot me a questioning glance and then changed the subject. "Well, this sure is a lot of food. Hana had time to bring it to the pet boutique on a Friday night? That can't be good news for her restaurant."

I helped myself to one of the volcano rolls. "No, actually Oggie brought it, and he said Happi Sushi is doing great. Apparently being accused of poisoning someone isn't a deterrent. Who knew?" I took the plate of California rolls Willow passed to me, ignoring the irony of us also eating Hana's food. "How did the interview go with her former business partner, Phil what's-his-name?"

Will spooned some noodles on his plate. "Not sure. He was a hard guy to read. He admitted he was at the seafood festival, but said it was out of curiosity. That he wanted to see the woman who single-handedly destroyed his investment in Kabuto Grill. Also, he's apparently known Hana for years, was a friend of her father's before he passed, and said the same thing as Oggie about her. That she'd never hurt someone else, only herself. He also denied having any involvement in Russo's death."

"Has anyone ever admitted committing murder without hard evidence against them?" Willow asked, her voice full of genuine curiosity.

Will wiped his mouth with a napkin and nodded. "You'd be surprised how much criminals want to tell you. Whether it's a guilty conscious or just bragging... people like to talk."

"But they also like to lie," I said. "Like Ren and Mr. Kam. Oh, Mr. Kam's daughter came into the boutique to get some flower essence for Rocky. Guess who her boyfriend is?"

Will set his chopsticks down. "Let me guess. Ren Tanaka?"

"Bingo. And she said Ren and Mr. Kam are still buddy-buddy, even play golf together all the time."

Will pursed his lips. "Interesting. All right, I'll see if I can get them both to voluntarily give their prints, in case we get something from the wine bottle or note."

"What if they won't agree to give them voluntarily?" Mallory asked.

"We have our ways." Will winked at her.

She grinned before shoving a California roll into her mouth.

I smiled to myself, enjoying their camaraderie. "When will you get the results back from the wine bottle and note?"

"The lab is putting a rush on it for us. So, hopefully just a day or two."

After we all stuffed ourselves, I helped Mallory clear the table. We carried everything into the kitchen, and Willow started loading the dishwasher.

As I cleaned up some noodles off the glass table, Will approached Grandma Winters. "Can I speak to you on the balcony?"

Wordlessly, she handed me the cloth napkins she'd been gathering and led the way.

Mallory raised an eyebrow at me over the kitchen counter as the two of them walked out onto the balcony, shutting the French doors behind them.

With worry tightening my chest, I carried the napkins into the kitchen. "That's weird, right?"

Willow leaned over the counter. We all watched them. "Looks serious." Willow said. "Will didn't tell you what he wanted to talk to her about?"

"No, I have no idea."

The balcony light was on so we could see them clearly. Will was doing the talking, his arms crossed, while Grandma Winters had her hands clasped in front of her, nodding occasionally. Goldie went and scratched at the door, not one to be left out. Their heads turned our way. We all scrambled to get back in the kitchen, just like when we were kids trying to eavesdrop on Mom's and Grandma's conversations.

Mallory shot me a disapproving glance. "Bet it has something to do with Zach hanging around you all the time. He's probably asking her what's going on between you two."

I rolled my eyes and busied myself with pulling out glass containers for the leftovers. Whatever they were talking about, I'm sure it had nothing to do with Zach. Well, maybe not one hundred percent sure.

When they came back in, Will looked pensive. Maybe even a bit worried. He stared into my eyes a bit longer than usual at the elevator. "I've got a few things to take care of tomorrow. Including helping Cynthia move that stuff out of her garage."

"Oh yeah." Was that what he was talking to Grandma Winters about? Was he having second thoughts about us and wanted some advice on letting me down easy? I should just ask, but I was too scared of what he'd say.

Will lifted my chin with his index finger until we were eye to eye. "Hey, you have nothing to worry about."

"Of course. I know." *But did I?* My insides were roiling, tears were threatening to surface, and I had no idea why. My world suddenly felt unstable.

"I'll call you when everything's wrapped up." With one last kiss, he disappeared behind the elevator door.

Petey scrambled over and yipped at the closing door, something he'd picked up from Daisy. I scooped him up and went to get Goldie's leash.

Grandma Winters approached me. Her expression was unreadable, but her eyes were unusually bright. "How much does Will know about your father and the gifts you girls got from him?"

I stared at her. Is that what Will had talked to her about? Was he not as comfortable with my visions as he'd let on? "Not... not much," I stuttered.

"I mean, I tried to explain my water magick to him at one point, but that didn't go so well. We're kind of at a don't-ask-don't-tell impasse."

She reached out and squeezed my hand. It alarmed me because she rarely showed physical affection. "I know it's been hard for you girls, being judged your whole lives for being different. And I know I've encouraged you to keep your gifts hidden. But, it's time to tell Will everything. If he truly loves you, he'll accept all of you."

I stared at her, my heart pounding. "And if he doesn't?"

She lifted her small chin. "Then it's better to know now."

※　※　※

"Stop biting your nails," Willow said, pulling my hand from my mouth. "And stop imagining the worst-case scenario."

I sighed. She was right. I had Will and Cynthia making out on her couch, confessing their undying love to each other. It was ridiculous. I trusted Will. I just didn't trust Cynthia not to try to win him back. "Fine. I'm gonna go take all this angst and get the inventory started."

The day moved slower than a three-legged turtle. I kept checking my phone but no call from Will. When the afternoon storms rolled around, I stood out on the sidewalk and connected to the rain, soothing my troubled heart and mind.

When Will finally called around four o'clock, I fumbled and dropped my phone twice before I answered it, heart racing. "Hey," I said, trying to sound nonchalant. "What's up? How's your day going? Things go okay?" I squeezed my eyes and lips shut.

Good grief, Darwin.

"Busy. Good news, though."

Cynthia has decided to move back to Germany?

"The wine bottle tested positive for TTX. So, we now know where the poison came from. Also, they pulled prints from the bottle and got a match. A guy named Timothy Rocheck. He's got a record for petty theft, drug charges. The problem is, his last known address is two years old. I'm wondering if that's because he's homeless now. I feel like I've seen him somewhere before but can't place him. Hang on."

I waited as Will had a short, muffled exchange with someone. "Sorry," he said. "Anyway, could you do me a favor and mention the name to Frankie? See if this guy's been through the homeless camp by any chance."

"Sure, no problem." I wanted to be happy about the new lead, but my brain was obsessing over Cynthia. I stared at the ceiling, forbidding myself from asking about her. It'd probably be better to hear about it in person anyway. "Want to grab some dinner tonight?"

"I do. But I've still got to interview Ren Tanaka. He's agreed to come to the station at six. Kam claims he's too busy, and I don't have enough evidence against him right now to arrest him. Especially in light of the new evidence pointing to this Rocheck guy. I'll call you when I'm finished. How's your day been?"

"Good. Fine. Summer is a bit slower, so I just have Mallory helping me out today. Charlie did a few baths, but everybody's chompin' at the bit for Sylvia to get back."

Frankie came through the door and folded up her dripping umbrella. Goldie pranced over and greeted Itty and Bitty as Frankie let them out of the carrier.

"Oh, speak of the devil, Frankie just walked in."

"Good timing. Let me know what she says," Will said. "I'll call you later. Love you."

"Love you, too."

"That was Will, I hope," Frankie teased.

I shot her a distracted smile. Now I had to wait even longer to find out what'd happened at Cynthia's place.

Frankie fluffed up her freshly dyed, bright red hair and eyed me. "What's wrong, sugar? You look worried about something."

I pulled out two tiny peanut butter treats for her dogs. "Not worried, no. Just distracted." I grabbed Goldie's collar as she tried to help the two dogs lick the crumbs off the floor. "Will wanted me to ask you if you recognize the name Timothy Rocheck. From Pirate City, maybe?"

"Rocheck," Frankie repeated.

I released Goldie. "Yeah, turns out the pufferfish poison was in the wine someone gave Ruth Russo. They pulled this Rocheck guy's prints off the bottle. His last known address is two years old, though, so Will figures maybe the guy is homeless now. Name ring a bell?"

"Darwin, did we get that specialty food in for Mr. Wilson's cats?" Mallory asked as she emerged from the cat food aisle.

"Yeah, it's in the storage closet, right hand side on the floor." I turned back to Frankie and was about to apologize for not having any human treats around. That was Sylvia's department. But Frankie was standing there, white as a sheet. "Frankie?"

She still didn't move. Her eyes looked right through me.

"Frankie? Are you all right?"

"Yeah," she croaked. "It's just... I do know Timothy Rocheck, and I know where he is."

CHAPTER SEVENTEEN

After I'd closed up the boutique and sent Goldie upstairs with Mal, Frankie and I rushed to meet Will at the hospital. We stood in the antiseptic-smelling hallway, outside Spider's room while Frankie filled Will in on what she knew about Spider, aka Timothy Rocheck.

Frankie was still pale and shaking her head in disbelief. "I mean, what motive would he have? He was an appliance repair guy before addiction got him, for heaven's sake. I doubt he even knew or cared who Ruth Russo was. It just doesn't make any sense. Why on earth would he poison her?"

I had to agree with her. "And where would he even get TTX in the first place? I doubt he has a medical license."

"These are all good questions," Will said, his arms crossed tightly against his chest. "And unfortunately, can only be answered by Mr. Rocheck."

A doctor with curly, gray hair and a clipped gate approached us. He held out a hand to Will. "Dr. Martinez. What can I help you with, Detective?"

"I need to question Mr. Rocheck. Is he in good enough health to handle that?"

Dr. Martinez shoved his hands in his white coat pockets. "Well, he's been in and out of consciousness the past twenty-four hours. Hasn't spoken yet, so I'm not sure how much you're going to get out of him." He glanced at me and Frankie. "Just one person should go in. His brain is damaged and can't handle too much stimulation. Please keep it short."

Will nodded. "I will. Thank you."

After only five minutes, Will emerged from the room. The corners of his mouth were turned down in disappointment.

"Nothing?" I asked.

"Nothing." Will rubbed the back of his neck roughly. "He opened his eyes once, but I couldn't connect with him. Then he was out again."

"You know, Will, I've been thinking." Frankie's face finally had some color. "There's only one thing that would make sense here. And that's if someone else got Spider to give Ruth Russo the wine and note. Like gave him money to deliver it. He was out of my sight for a bit at the seafood festival. Someone could've paid him to do it then. That would also explain how Spider got money for the heroin he overdosed on."

Will's hands were resting lightly on his hips, his head lowered in thought. "Yeah. That's a definite possibility."

"Good thinking, Frankie," I said.

Will glanced at his phone. "I need to go find Dr. Martinez, ask him to let me know as soon as Rocheck is coherent enough to look at some suspect photos. Then, I need to get back to the station to meet Ren Tanaka. I still want to know why he lied about his relationship with Mr. Kam." He turned to me and rubbed my arms. "If it's not too late when I'm done, you want me to swing by with some takeout?"

My heart did a little tap dance in my chest as I remembered his visit to Cynthia's today. "Yes, please." I'd never be able to fall asleep if I didn't find out what had happened.

❈ ❈ ❈

When Will showed up around eight o'clock, my family made themselves scarce. Tonight I was planning on trying to explain our elemental magick to Will. I still wasn't so sure it was a good idea, but I trusted Grandma Winters's judgment, and she insisted it was time.

"Hey." I gave Will a quick kiss and then led him into the kitchen to put down the two brown bags of take-out he was cradling in his arms.

Goldie turned circles in front of Will, slowing him down. I wasn't sure if she was excited about his visit or the mouth-watering smells wafting from the bags. "Goldie, move, girl. Chinese *and* Italian? Are we feeding the neighborhood tonight?" I teased him.

He plopped the bags down on the counter, then ruffled Goldie's ears. "I brought enough for your sisters and Grandma. Wasn't sure what they liked. Not for you," he said affectionately to Goldie. Then glancing around, "Where is everyone?"

"Oh, Mallory took Petey and Lucky upstairs with her. She's working on her online classes. Willow and Grandma Winters went to dinner with Jade and Kimi, so it's just us and Goldie tonight."

"Is that so?" He pulled me into his arms, a slow, devilish grin appearing. "Whatever shall we do?"

My stomach contracted, then sank, as I thought about the conversation we were going to have. Lifting my chin, I forced cheer into my words. "First we should eat before this feast gets cold."

A soft, growling noise rumbled in his chest, then he placed a warm kiss on my lips. "To be continued then."

We settled onto the sofa with our takeout. Lightning flashed outside the French doors, followed by distant thunder. Muffled music drifted up from the sidewalk band below.

"So, did Ren Tanaka show up at the station?" I asked, pulling the lid off the steaming eggplant pasta bake.

"He did, with his lawyer in tow." Will accepted a plate after I'd spooned a big cheesy, gooey slice onto it. "Thanks. Tanaka still insists he wasn't at the seafood festival, though he doesn't have an alibi, either. Says he was home alone all day."

I licked tomato sauce off my finger. "You know, you could ask his nosey neighbor across the street to verify that. Bet she would know. She's the one who told me about Mr. Kam and Rocky being at Ren's house on Sunday."

Will's fork stopped halfway to his mouth and he raised a brow. "I'm going to ignore the fact that you went back and talked to her on your own."

"Sorry," I said, grinning. "Won't happen again."

"Yeah, right." Will tried to look stern but failed miserably. "Anyway, after I told Tanaka I knew he was dating Kam's daughter—and still plays golf with Mr. Kam regularly—he confessed to going to work for Hana at Mr. Kam's request."

I almost choked on my mouthful of food. After coughing and swallowing, I said, "He admitted that? With his lawyer there?"

Will handed me a glass of water. "Yeah and his lawyer wasn't too pleased about it, either. But Tanaka said he was coming clean about why he went to work at Happi Sushi because he didn't have anything to do with Russo's death, and he didn't want to be blamed for that."

I set the glass back down on the coffee table and cleared my throat. "So, Mr. Kam didn't fire him after all? He just wanted Ren to go work for Hana to do what? Sabotage her restaurant somehow, like Oggie thought?"

"According to Tanaka, their plan was just to talk Hana into making some menu changes that wouldn't be particularly helpful. Though, I need to talk to Mr. Kam to see if his story is the same."

I pushed my food around, suddenly not hungry. "It seems like Ren's throwing Mr. Kam—his friend and girlfriend's father—under the bus. Why would he do that?"

Will pointed his fork at me. "Good question. When I asked that very same thing, Tanaka said Kam wouldn't want it to get out that he tried to sabotage Hana's business. It'd ruin his reputation, so he'd never admit to it. But Tanaka insists Kam didn't have anything to do with poisoning Russo, either. So, he figured if he explained their actual plan, I'd understand it wasn't anything close to murder."

Goldie inched forward to lay her chin on my bare toe, eyes locked on my plate. She sensed my weakness. I pinched off a tiny bit of cheese and gave it to her. I was creating a cheese monster, I knew, but I couldn't resist those pleading eyes. "So, do you believe Ren? That neither of them had anything to do with the poisoning?"

Will swallowed and wiped his mouth with a napkin. "I believe facts, and the fact is Mr. Kam was at the seafood festival and so had both motive and opportunity. And now that we suspect someone paid Timothy Rocheck to deliver the wine, Kam wouldn't even have had to leave his booth to poison her."

A strobe of lightning flashed outside, thunder right on its heels. A heavy rain began to fall. A sense of peace flowed through me. I set my plate down and relaxed against Will's arm, thinking. "Mr. Kam also has a license to order fugu. Though he said he hadn't ordered any from Wako International in four years and you verified that."

Goldie gave up begging for more cheese, grabbed Gator and plopped down in front of the French doors to watch the storm.

Will ran a thumb over my hand sending chills up my arm. "Yeah, but like you said before, he could've kept some frozen from that order."

As his long fingers threaded through mine, I snuggled in closer. "If he did keep it frozen, could he have extracted the poison from it? Then served it to her in the wine, so she'd be the only one to ingest it?"

Will's other hand went to my hair, twirling a short strand around his finger. "It's a possibility.

The toxin is found in the fish's liver, intestines and ovaries. More than likely there's a way to extract it or maybe even just dry out those body parts and make a powder. I'll have to look into that. Remember they wouldn't need much to kill someone. I've got a judge working on a warrant to search Kam's restaurant."

I forced myself to sit up and out of Will's warm embrace. I was getting too comfortable, and we still had a long conversation ahead. "So, now that we believe someone paid Spider to deliver the poisoned wine, don't you think Skip Pascoe should still be a suspect? He did have motive, opportunity and wouldn't have had to leave his booth, either."

Will reached for his water glass. "True, but we compared the handwriting on the note delivered with the wine to the one Pascoe had left on Russo's car. It wasn't a match. I'll add Pascoe's photo to the ones I take to have Mr. Rocheck look at, just to be sure. Though, I can't see any way he'd have access to TTX, either." He sighed and picked up a fortune cookie. "I hope Rocheck will be cognizant enough to give us some answers soon."

Will started to unwrap the cookie, bringing Goldie scrambling over to sit in front of him. Her brows twitched as she alternated her best pleading look between Will and the cookie. Will broke it in half and held it out to her.

"You're such a pushover," I said, as Goldie gently took it from his palm, tail swishing happily.

Pot calling the kettle black, I know.

"What a coincidence." Will held the strip of paper from the cookie between his fingers and grinned. "That's exactly what my fortune says."

"Really?" I asked skeptically.

"No." He chuckled. "Actually, I like this one. It says, 'Life is not a problem to be solved, but a mystery to be lived'."

"Well, right now it's a mystery to be solved," I said, unwrapping my own cookie.

I glanced at Goldie, who was licking her chops. "Don't even think about it. You already got one." She picked up Gator and play bowed, like she wasn't really thinking about it, fooling exactly no one. "Mine says, 'never forget that a half truth is a whole lie'."

I crumbled up the tiny paper and shoved the cookie in my mouth. I wanted to shove the paper in my mouth, too, and make it disappear. *Thanks, Universe.* The guilt one little cookie could induce was surprisingly strong.

Will took a sip of his water and then pulled my feet onto his lap. "So, I haven't got a chance to tell you about going over to Cynthia's." His skilled hands went to work massaging all the stress out of my feet as he talked. "You were right. She had this idea that she could come back here and pick up where we left off. Had this whole candlelit dinner thing on the table when I got there. It really took me by surprise."

I glanced over at our water glasses, proud of myself for not losing control of my magick as dark feelings of anger and jealousy pulsed in my veins. Tuning into the rain, I allowed the strong emotional energy to flow out of my body. My voice was surprisingly even as I asked, "That must've been really awkward. How did you handle it?" Maybe it was all the practice I'd been doing keeping me calm. Or maybe it was the foot massage.

Will moved his hands up to my bare ankles. "Well, I asked her to point me to the stuff she needed moved. Then she admitted there wasn't anything. That she just wanted to talk. I told her that we had nothing to talk about. She got really upset. Said she moved back here to give us another shot. Can you believe that? I mean the audacity." He shook his head and a wave of his anger washed over and through me. I stayed silent and let him talk. "I told her I was in a relationship and very happy. Then I wished the same for her and left."

I watched the shifting emotions play out on his expression. Well, he's happy now. How will he feel when I tell him the whole truth about my father and our elemental magick? He probably won't be so happy then. Could that kind of news push him back into Cynthia's arms?

"I'm sorry you had to go through that, Will. That must've been really confusing."

His eyes met mine quickly. "No, not confusing at all. I meant what I said. I'm a happy man. Come here." He pulled me forward into his chest. My arms wrapped around him, his chin resting on my head. "Are you happy, too?" he asked, a touch of concern in his voice.

I raised my gaze to meet his. "Of course." I pushed myself up and sighed. It was time. "But I do need to explain some things to you that might affect how happy you are with me."

He kissed my forehead. "You can tell me anything. Nothing will change the way I feel about you."

"Remember you said that." I rested my hand on his heart. "Listen from here, please. Not from your analytical detective mind."

He covered my hand with his and rubbed the amethyst ring on my finger. "I made a promise to try my best, remember?"

I bit my lip. "I do." *Here goes nothing then.* "Do you remember how I told you that I could add properties to water?"

His expression stayed neutral, but his chest rose with a deep, steadying breath. I knew taking him back to the time he thought I'd betrayed him was probably not the best idea, but it had to be done. He was bracing himself. "Yes."

"Well, it's called elemental magick, and my whole family is blessed—or cursed—with it, depending on how you look at it."

Will's brow wrinkled; his eyes registered confusion. He needed some solid evidence, some facts to latch onto.

What will convince him?

I grabbed his hand. "Remember the airport incident with the fire? And I said you wouldn't be able to put it in your report, if I told you what had really happened?"

His gaze fell to the floor as he remembered. "Yes."

I waited until he looked at me again. "Well, that was because Mallory started that fire with her magick. She can control fire. Willow can control elements of earth. And this is because our father isn't human, he's an Elemental."

Will was watching my eyes carefully. Maybe trying to figure out if I was pulling his leg. He was still listening, though—or at least stunned into silence—so I kept going, spilling everything I knew about our family history, Grandma Winters, the things we could do with our magick, how I had shunned it to try to be normal, and about how Father was now Iris's prisoner.

And that brought me to Zach.

I placed a hand on my stomach to settle down the churning. "You wanted to know what Zach was doing here. Well, that has to do with our father. Zach is a hybrid, too. Only he's not Elemental, he's jinn."

"Like a genie?" Will said, half-laughing but his face had paled. Somewhere deep down he was beginning to believe the world might not be as black and white as he saw it.

I nodded solemnly. "Because of this, Grandma Winters has asked him to come with me as protection to the Otherworld to rescue Father."

"Wow." Will moved his gaze from my face to stare at the French doors. A particularly loud round of thunder and burst of lightning hit.

I watched every flicker of emotion from fear to hope cross his face. "Will, tell me what you're thinking."

His voice was soft, but void of emotion, like he was in a trance. "I mean, I'm trying not to think. But to just accept what you're telling me. Obviously, you believe it."

Is he in shock?

I sat up and grabbed my water glass. His analytical detective mind needed undeniable proof. He needed to see it with his own eyes. "Hold this."

When the glass was firmly in his hand, I moved my energy into resonance with the water. It immediately reacted and began a slow swirl clockwise. I glanced at Will. He was staring at the water, his face pale, his mouth open. I sped it up until it was a vortex almost hitting the top rim. Will glanced from the glass to me a few times and then quickly set the glass down with a shaky hand. He rubbed his hands on his jeans and watched as I let the water settle back down. Then he fell back into the sofa and raked a hand over his face.

I gave him a minute to process.

He finally looked at me, grinned and then began to laugh. And I mean, a big ol' belly rumbling, face-reddening, knee-slapping laugh. He wiped at his eyes with the back of his hand.

I eyed him suspiciously. *Did I break him?* "You all right?"

He nodded, still getting himself under control. "Sorry. I can't even explain what I'm feeling right now. Though, I'm not laughing at you." He stood and went to the French doors, hands on his hips as he stared at the storm. Goldie joined him, looking up at him, wondering if he was going to open the doors.

I was dying to know what he was thinking but didn't dare disturb him. He obviously needed some space.

I started gathering our plates and takeout boxes from the coffee table and carried them to the kitchen. While I was in there, I put on a pot of water for tea. Grandma Winters would've just heated it up with her hands if no one was looking. It was the first time we'd seen Grandma Winters outside our Savannah house, interacting with the world, and she used her magick like it was just an extension of herself. Nothing noticeable to others, but we saw the way she'd manipulate a traffic light or a rain cloud. She was capable of much more of course, but she was careful not to upset the balance of our world.

By the time I had everything cleaned up and carried the two cups of steaming chamomile tea to the living room, Will was sitting back on the sofa.

Well, he hadn't hightailed it out of here, that's a good sign.

I glanced at him cautiously. His eyes were a bit glassy, but his expression was calm. He seemed to be in deep contemplation. I folded my hands around the warm cup and waited.

Finally, he spoke, though he was still staring at the floor. "I don't consider myself the most intelligent person in the world, but I did pride myself on only believing what I could prove. I believed something to be true when I had facts to back it up. That's what my whole profession is based on. Well, maybe some intuitive hunches occasionally but then again... facts had to back up those hunches."

He finally looked at me, cocking his head like he was seeing me for the first time. "You've completely turned my world upside down. There are things out there I will never understand, obviously. Things that would be beyond belief if I didn't see them with my own eyes. I mean... magic? You wouldn't have convinced me in a million years that magic was real. But here you are. Sitting in front of me. Showing me magic is real. And I'm feeling like a complete idiot for closing my mind to everything except what I could see and touch. Closing my mind to faith." His eyes were damp with unshed tears. "I have a lot to reconsider about my beliefs and where they come from. If I had to say where they came from, I'd say fear. The need to control my environment. When my brother was killed, I lost faith in everything. The world stopped making sense. It lost its color. It lost its... magic. Anyway, I'm not even sure what I'm trying to say." He shook his head and reached for my hand. "Except this: I know how hard it must've been for you to be honest with me about your family gifts, to open up, knowing how skeptical I am. Thank you for trusting me enough to tell me the truth."

I jumped into his arms with a gasp. *Could it be this easy?* I squeezed his neck, tears running down my face and dropping onto his collarbone. "Thank you for believing me," I whispered through the tears. A heavy weight lifted off my chest and I felt dizzy with joy and relief. "Thank you, thank you, thank you."

He squeezed me tighter.

Goldie jumped up on the sofa and shoved her nose in between us with a whimper. Laughing, we both rubbed her neck and then Will was kissing my cheeks, my neck, my lips. Goldie nudged us apart again and pawed at Will's hand.

"Goldie!" I laughed, throwing a hand up to protect my face from her long tongue. She just couldn't help herself, she had to get in on the celebration.

The elevator door slid opened, sending Willow's soft laughter echoing through the house.

Grandma Winters and Willow stepped out. Goldie jumped down to greet them while Will and I untangled ourselves to join her.

Mallory must've also heard them come in. She padded down the stairs with Lucky in her arms. I knew she was dying to know how my conversation with Will had gone.

"How was dinner?" I asked Willow as she stroked Goldie's muzzle.

"It was fun," Willow answered, glancing from me to Will. "Yours?"

"Great. Perfect." I glanced up at Will, joy still lighting me up inside. "We had a great talk."

"So, Will knows everything?" Grandma Winters asked.

"Do I?" Will teased, slipping his arm around me.

"Yes!" I laughed. Then, looking back at Grandma Winters, "Yes, I told him everything."

She eyed Will. "And yet he stays." She flicked her chin toward the elevator while holding eye contact with Will. "Then I'll walk you out."

"Guess I'm leaving," Will said, planting a kiss on both my cheeks. "See you tomorrow."

After the door closed, I whirled around and stared at my sisters. "Why is she walking Will out? That's odd, right?"

They shared a concerned look. Then Mallory stared at me with something resembling pity. "I wish I could say you're just being paranoid, but yeah... that's strange."

CHAPTER EIGHTEEN

Sunday morning, Mallory and I were helping Frankie out with breakfast for the homeless. The grass at Mirror Park was still damp with last night's rain. I was on the proverbial cloud nine because of Will's positive reaction last night and could not keep the grin off my face. Life could not get any shinier or sweeter.

"Hey, there, Snow White." Mac greeted me with a salute.

"Hey there yourself," I said, squinting into the sunshine. "How's things?"

"Can't complain. It's a beautiful day to be alive." He winked as he accepted the plate full of scrambled eggs and orange slices.

"You got that right, sugar," Frankie said beside me. With her tongs, she dropped a bagel on his plate. "Any day's a good day on this side of the dirt."

Mac chuckled. "Speakin' of. How's Spider doin'? You seen him lately?" He stepped back to let the next person get a bagel.

Frankie shook her head. "Still pretty out of it, far as I know. The hospital's supposed to call me if he gets to the point where he's conscious for more than a few seconds."

Mac grunted and adjusted his ratty ball cap. "I'm really sorry, Frankie. I tried to keep an eye on him."

Frankie waved a plastic-gloved hand. "Don't beat yourself up. You of all people should know you can't save everybody."

"Hi, nice cookie lady!" G stood in front of me with a grin.

"Hey, G," I said, surprised. I hadn't seen him for a few weeks.

He pulled his hand out from behind his back and handed me a wilted dandelion.

"Is this for me? Well, how'd you know yellow is my favorite color?" I tucked the flower behind my ear and grinned at him. "Thank you kindly. Wasn't sure you were going to be here today." I reached in my bag under the table and pulled out a baggie of peanut butter cookies. "But I took a chance."

His yellowed eyes squinted with pleasure as I handed him the bag. "Yeah. My favorite. These are my favorite. Thanks."

"You're welcome," I said, handing him a plate of eggs, too. "You take care now."

"You sure do have a lot of nicknames around here," Mallory said. She was sitting on a trash bag to keep her backside dry, peeling the oranges and pulling the slices apart. The citrus scent mingled in the air with the buttery eggs. Surprisingly, she wasn't teasing me, but instead looking up at me with—dare I say?—admiration.

I pushed a stray wave out of my face with the back of my gloved hand. "Don't worry, you hang around here long enough, you'll get a few of your own." I handed out another plate. "Here ya go."

Then glanced back down at Mallory. "So, have you seriously considered staying here?"

Without taking her eyes from the half-peeled orange in her hand, she asked, "Do you really want me to?"

I spooned some eggs onto a plate, frowning. "Of course. Why ever wouldn't I?" In her silence, I understood her insecurity. "Look, Mal. When I left Savannah, I didn't leave y'all. I just wanted to start over in a town that didn't know me or shun me. I'm really happy you and Willow are here now, and I'd like you both to stay. I know you're gonna be looking for a graphic design job in the future, but meanwhile your help at the pet boutique has been invaluable. Plus, we have the new shelter opening up. There's going to be a ton of work for that. I need you here." I glanced down to gauge her reaction.

She wore a suppressed smirk. "You *need* me?"

I waited until she looked up at me, so she'd know I was serious. "Yes, and I *want* you here."

Her smile and nod gave me warm fuzzies. I think she finally understood why I'd left or at least forgave me for it.

Frankie and I were loading the silver buffet servers back in her van when she got a call.

"This is Frankie," she said, squishing the phone between her chin and shoulder as she maneuvered the buffet server into place. "Really? Great news. Thank you." She slid her phone back in her pocket and gave me a thumb's up. "Wahoo. Seems Spider is finally responding and able to stay conscious for a bit."

"Does that mean he's out of the woods?" I asked.

She shrugged. "Don't think he'll ever really be out of the woods. But this battle may be won." She glanced back at Mallory, who was taking a trash bag around to gather everyone's plates. "I'm gonna head over there. You want to come?"

I probably should. They'd be calling Will, too, I assumed. Mal and I had ridden our bikes here, but I don't think she'd mind riding back alone. I glanced in the back of the van. "Can you fit my bike back here?"

"Sure. Go grab it."

I was right. By the time we arrived, Will was already talking to Dr. Martinez outside Spider's door. We waited until they were done and then approached him.

"Hey." He was dressed in jeans and a light blue polo shirt, his detective badge clipped to his pocket and a folder clutched in his hand. "Mr. Rocheck's apparently awake right now, though still not talking much. I'm going to head in first if you don't mind, Frankie."

"Not at all," she said, waving toward the door. "Darwin, why don't you go on in with him. I'll go grab us some coffee."

I gave Will a questioning look. "Can I? I'll just be in the corner, observing."

He nodded, already distracted, as he pushed through the door.

Spider was just a pale face lost in white pillows and sheets. Machines beeped beside him, wires running from each machine and disappearing beneath the covers. He did have his eyes cracked open, though and they followed us as we entered the room. I took a seat in the corner as Will pulled up a chair to his bed.

"Good afternoon, Mr. Rocheck. I don't know if you remember me. Detective Will Blake? We met briefly at the seafood festival."

Spider swallowed, but it was the only movement.

Will continued, his tone soft and unhurried. "That day one of the judges, Ruth Russo, got real sick. Can you blink if you were aware of that?"

Spider's eyes closed for a few seconds, then he opened them and watched Will expectantly.

Will nodded with a soft smile. "Good. That's real helpful. Now, here's the thing. We've since learned that Ms. Russo was poisoned." Will paused, probably looking for any reaction from Spider. Then continued when he didn't get one. "It turns out that poison came from a wine bottle that was delivered to Ms. Russo with a note that said, 'for all you do'. Does that ring a bell?"

This time even I could see the reaction on Spider's face from my vantage point. His eyes widened, and his mouth dropped open. An eerie moan escaped his throat.

Will leaned closer. "You delivered that wine to Ms. Russo, didn't you? You can blink once for yes."

Spider's eyes shut tight and popped back open. He looked distressed.

Will held up his hand. "You're not in trouble. I believe someone gave you money in exchange for delivering the wine to Ms. Russo. Is that what happened?"

Spider squeezed his eyes shut and opened them wide. His tongue working in his dry mouth like he was trying to get words out.

Will pulled out the photos from the folder. "I'm going to show you a few photos, and I want you to blink if one of them is the person who paid you to deliver the wine. Can you do that?"

Spider blinked hard. Then his eyes stayed on Will's face.

Will held out the first photo. It was a blown-up copy of Skip Pascoe's driver's license. Spider stared at the photo then moved his gaze back to Will without blinking.

Will nodded and slipped it back into the folder.

Guess Skip Pascoe was off the hook.

The next photo was of Phil Cunningham, Hana's ex business partner. Spider didn't blink. He was starting to look real tired, though.

Will showed him a photo of Ren Tanaka. No reaction.

Placing that one behind the others, Will held up the next photo. It was Mr. Kam. Will watched Spider expectantly, his back stiff, his body very still. "Is this the person who paid you to deliver the wine?"

Spider moved his eyes from the photo to Will. He didn't blink.

Will glanced over at me. "You're doing great. One last one." He held up a picture of Hana.

I held my breath. Spider stared at it for a long few seconds. Then his eyes moved slowly to Will. No blink.

Will's shoulders fell. "All right. Thanks for your help. You should rest now. I'll see you soon."

Spider's eyes were closed before we even left the room. My heart broke for him. Such a long road of recovery ahead.

We stepped out of the room and Will blew out a deep breath.

I slid my arm around his waist. "Well, that wasn't very productive."

Frankie walked up and handed us each a coffee cup from a cardboard carrier. "How'd it go?"

"Thanks." Will said, accepting the cup. "He still isn't talking but could communicate with me a bit through blinking."

Frankie's lips pursed. "Guess that's something. Did he ID the person who paid him to deliver the wine?"

"No." Will tapped the folder against his leg. "Maybe I didn't have the right person to show him, or maybe his brain's too damaged to remember. Anyway, he's resting now."

"Well, shoot, sorry. I'm just going to peek in on him then." To me she asked, "You catchin' a ride home with Will?"

I tilted my face up to Will. He nodded. "Sure, I'll just grab my bike tomorrow."

❈　❈　❈

Will started the car. "You feel like an early dinner?"

I smirked. "Sushi at Kam's?"

His eyes sparkled with humor, even in the dim light of the hospital parking garage. "And she's smart, too." Leaning over with a chuckle, he planted a kiss on my lips. "How'd I get so lucky?"

I bit my lip playfully. "Maybe I put a spell on you."

Will's head whipped back to me. He looked so horrified, I burst out laughing. "Relax, Detective. I can't do that."

He shook his head. Turning the wheel, he shot me a chastising look that quickly morphed into a suppressed smile. "Too early to joke about that."

"Sorry," I said, stifling a second round of laughter. "Won't happen again."

This forced a deep chuckle from his chest as he accelerated onto the street.

Mr. Kam did not seem pleased to see Will in his restaurant. He made a beeline to our table not two minutes after we were seated, wringing his hands nervously. "Detective Blake. May I suggest the fresh tuna ceviche for your dining pleasure this evening." He glanced around the half-full dining room. "Can I get you a bottle of our house wine?"

Will's brow raised. "It's not the Chateau Ste. Veuve, is it?"

Mr. Kam's face blanched. "No, no, of course not." His vocal cords tightened, sending his voice soaring. "Good joke. Good one. Is there anything else I can get you?"

Will unclipped his badge and tossed it onto the table with a loud clunk. People at the nearby tables glanced over.

Mr. Kam stiffened.

"Seeing how you're too busy to come to the station for a chat, I guess we can do it here. Have a seat," Will commanded, pointing to the empty chair beside me.

Mr. Kam slid down into it like he wanted to keep going and melt into the floor.

"I've learned something interesting recently. Seems your daughter is dating Ren Tanaka." He let that sit between them for a moment, hands folded casually on the table.

Mr. Kam was squirming beside me. I could hardly pay attention to him though, because Will just looked so darned handsome when he was digging for the truth. Square jaw set, blue eyes burning with a cool fire. *Swoon.*

"Yes, I guess they date," Mr. Kam finally admitted.

"Tell me the real reason you sent your daughter's boyfriend to work for Happi Sushi." Will's assured demeanor left no room for doubt that he already knew the answer.

Mr. Kam held up his hands. "Sent him? What do you mean sent him? I don't control where people work."

Will just kept staring at Mr. Kam while the man wound himself from indignation to frustration to finally slumping in surrender. "Fine. I just wanted him to, you know, make some menu changes so Happy Sushi doesn't keep all my customers. I know what sells in this area and want to make sure people are buying it here. I did not send him to poison *anyone.*"

Will leaned forward. "Is that what you think happened? You think Ren Tanaka poisoned Ms. Russo?"

His hands whirled around. "Why would he do that?"

"Good question."

Mr. Kam started shaking his head vehemently. "I did not tell him to do that."

"No?" Will said, leaning casually back. "I mean, it would be a smart plan. Frame your competition for murder, get her out of the way completely. Smarter than just a few menu changes that may or may not be effective. Are you a smart man, Mr. Kam?"

He was still shaking his head. "No. I'm not. I'm not a smart man."

Will's head tilted sympathetically. "I don't think you're giving yourself enough credit."

Mr. Kam rubbed his face. "I don't think I should say anything else without my lawyer."

"Okay." Will picked his badge up and knocked it on the table a few times. "Have your lawyer call the station tomorrow morning to set up a formal interview. Bright and early. I'll also need a writing sample while you're there."

Mr. Kam nodded and slipped out of the chair, head down.

Will watched him go and then reached across the table for my hand. "Now that business is out of the way, what do you say we forget about the investigation and just enjoy the rest of our Sunday?"

Will's phone buzzed in his pocket. He squeezed his eyes shut. "Or not."

I smiled and pulled the menu closer. "I am enjoying my Sunday."

He reluctantly released my hand. "Detective Blake."

I glanced up at Will when I noticed his silence. He was listening intently. "That so?" he finally said.

Taking out his notebook and pen, he started scribbling excitedly. "Thanks, and good work."

"Was that about the case?" I asked when he hung up.

He seemed pleasantly stunned as he stared at his phone for a moment. Then, sliding it back in his pocket, he met my gaze. "Yes, in fact, I think we just caught a big break. I've had officers making calls to online companies where someone could purchase TTX with a medical license, typically researchers at universities or pharmaceutical companies. I wanted to see if anyone shipped the toxin to our area recently. It was a complete fishing expedition— pardon the pun—because there's so many of these companies. But Officer Starks just got a hit on a company called VOC Bioscience, who says they shipped an order for one milligram to a P.O. Box here in St. Pete." He checked his notebook. "Sent to a Dr. Drew Trawets who claimed he represents a company called TD Research, Inc. Only Officer Starks can't find any record of the company or a Dr. Trawets."

Will's excitement was contagious. My skin tingled. "So, do you think this Trawets guy faked being a doctor somehow?"

"I'll have to see exactly what credentials VOC Bioscience required as proof of having a medical license. You'd think they'd make it pretty difficult to use fake credentials considering how dangerous the stuff is they're selling."

I stared at Will, trying to piece together how this fit into what we already knew. "When did they ship the TTX?"

He glanced down at his notepad. "August seventh. Two weeks before Ruth Russo was poisoned."

I quickly recalled our conversation with Oggie and with relief said, "Oggie told us Hana found out about Ruth Russo judging the contest on the eleventh, during their fight. That wouldn't have been enough time for Hana to figure out how to get fake doctor credentials and set up the P.O. Box."

"How do we know that's really when Hana found out? She told us the fight was because she accused Oggie of using drugs again." Will's stare held a new intensity. "Besides, she could've had all that set up in advance and was just waiting for the right opportunity to order the toxin. Waiting until she could see Ruth Russo in the flesh."

CHAPTER NINETEEN

Monday morning, I left Mal with Charlie to run the pet boutique while I had lunch a few doors down at the Parkshore Grill with Willow and Grandma Winters.

Goldie was resting in the shade under the table, her chin parked on my foot. It was a blazing hot afternoon with no breeze to speak of, so the restaurant was kind enough to have large fans running.

After the waitress took our order and filled up our water glasses, Grandma Winters turned to me. "I wanted to start firming up our plan for sending you and Zach to the Otherworld, but you look really distracted. You cannot be distracted when you go."

I lowered my eyes, my face warming from her disapproval. "I know." Forcing myself to meet her intimidating gaze, I explained, "It's just today could be a big turning point in the case. Will's text this morning said the search warrant came through, so they'll be searching Mr. Kam's restaurant while he and his lawyer are at the station for a formal interview." Grandma Winters's expression didn't soften, so I kept trying to explain why this was so important to me. "I've really grown to care about what happens to Hana and Daisy."

The table beside us broke out into laughter. A car horn sounded down the street. Still, Grandma Winters didn't take her eyes off me, her narrow mouth set in a hard line.

Thankfully Willow broke the awkward silence. "Does Will no longer consider Hana a suspect then?"

I turned to Willow, letting out the breath I'd been holding. "He hasn't ruled her out yet, unfortunately. He's just concentrating on Mr. Kam at the moment because he admitted to sending his sous-chef to work for Hana, to sabotage her menu. Which means Mr. Kam considered Happi Sushi more of a threat than he let on."

Willow scooted her chair in after someone bumped it trying to get by on the sidewalk. "Well, that's not very nice, but what does sabotaging Hana's menu have to do with Ruth Russo's murder?"

I twisted my water glass absentmindedly. "Will figures it wouldn't be that big of a leap from sabotage to poisoning Ruth Russo and framing Hana for it, killing two birds with one stone. Mr. Kam would be getting rid of his competition, while also getting rid of Ruth Russo before she could publish her review of Kam's, which Will found out was going to be real ugly."

Willow paused from slathering whipped butter on a piece of rye bread. Frown lines formed on her forehead. "That does sound like it would take care of Mr. Kam's problems, but I don't know. Murder is a big leap for anyone."

"If that were the case, Will would be out of a job." I dropped a couple of ice cubes from my glass into Goldie's water bowl. "Anyway, there's also some new information, and we can't figure out where it fits. Will got a lead on an order of TTX, the pufferfish toxin, that was sent to a P.O. Box here two weeks before Ruth Russo was poisoned. You'd need a medical license to order it, which Mr. Kam *doesn't* have."

"Wasn't there a record of who rented the P.O. Box?" Willow asked.

"There was a doctor's name and a company name, but neither of 'em seems to exist. Also, Mr. Kam does have a license to buy fugu legally, so if he is the killer, why wouldn't he just get the poison that way?"

"Maybe so it couldn't be traced back to him?"

Grandma Winters had been silently watching our exchange, but now she leaned forward on the table and folded her hands. Her pale green eyes glittered in the sunlight. "I think we should wait until this case is solved to rescue Ash."

Willow stopped chewing and glanced from me to Grandma Winters. "But you said we have to act soon, so Iris doesn't move Father again."

"No." I shook my head vehemently. "We don't have to wait, honest. I'm ready."

Grandma Winters stretched her neck to view the sidewalk crowd behind me. "Isn't that Will's ex-wife?"

My head whipped around, scanning the people passing by. "Is it? Where?" When I turned back, Grandma Winters had her attention focused on my water glass.

"Good," she said with a hint of a smile. "Your control under emotional distress is improving."

It took me a second to realize Cynthia wasn't there. Grandma Winters had been testing me to see if I'd lose control and slosh water all over the table. And thank the stars I'd passed.

Feeling a bit more confident, I met Grandma Winter's gaze. "I'm ready. And I'd like to invite Will to be there when we do this." I hadn't thought about it until that moment, but it suddenly seemed important for him to be there with me.

Willow rested a warm hand on my arm. "Are you sure you want to do that? Being told about our magick and seeing it in person are two very different things."

"I think it's an excellent idea," Grandma Winters said, relaxing back in her chair.

"You do?" Willow and I said in tandem.

"Yes." She stared at us silently, obviously not planning to explain further.

Willow and I shared a surprised look, and I wondered again what Will had wanted to talk to Grandma Winters about that day on the balcony.

❖ ❖ ❖

Just before closing time, the chime over the door jingled, and Ogden Stewart strolled in.

I glanced up from the counter. "Oh, hey Oggie."

Goldie and Petey had been curled up together under the table, watching the people pass by outside. They both ventured out to greet the long-haired white cat on the other end of the leash in Oggie's hand.

Shoving the birthday cake orders I'd been looking over back into the manila envelope, I rounded the counter. "And who do we have here?" The cat's sapphire blue eyes tracked me as I approached. "Hello, gorgeous."

"This is Princess. Hope it's okay I brought her in with me. She really enjoys getting out and about."

"Absolutely. And don't worry," I added when the dogs stretched their heads to get a closer sniff. "They're both good with cats."

Petey suddenly leapt forward with a sharp *ruff!* And play bowed, tail ticking back and forth. Princess's ears flattened and her paw struck out like lightning, bopping him on the nose. He barked again, apparently not discouraged by this new potential playmate's rebuff.

"Okay, no harassing our clientele." I scooped Petey up and cradled him in the crook of my arm. Goldie was smart enough to sit and watch Princess out of paw's reach, while the cat licked the paw she'd used to swat Petey. "So, what brings you and Princess in this evening?"

He glanced over the boutique aisles. "Hana wanted me to pick up some of those organic treats Daisy likes so much."

I adjusted Petey, who was squirming and trying to get back down on the floor. "Sure. I'll grab those for you. How's Daisy doing?"

"She's doing great. Hana, too." He followed me as I placed Petey in his gated pen. "Happi Sushi's been busy, so she's pleased."

"That's good to hear. Ren Tanaka still working there?" I slipped a small paper bag out from the stash beneath the treat display.

"Yeah. Is there a reason he shouldn't be?"

"Oh. I..." *Way to stick your foot in your mouth, Darwin.* "I just thought Hana might've considered what you'd said." I glanced at him sheepishly. "You know, that you never liked Ren. That he seemed shady." I couldn't divulge what Will had discovered about Ren's motives through his investigation. Maybe when this was all over, Will could have a talk with Hana about why Ren went to work for her. If he didn't quit first, which was pretty likely now. Time to change the subject. "By the way, we just got in some delicious freeze-dried chicken and salmon." I looked up from scooping the treats into the bag. "I mean, I haven't tried them myself, obviously. But our other cat clientele who are on special diets just go crazy over them."

Oggie was looking at me like I'd grown a second head. "Well, she's not on any kind of special diet," he finally said. "But I'm sure she'd find it a nice change from her regular food. She does love to eat."

We both glanced down at Princess, who was rubbing herself against Oggie's leg. Goldie was stretched out a few feet away, watching her in fascination.

Now I was the one who was confused. Maybe the vet hadn't thought Princess needed to switch to a special diet for her diabetes? Or maybe he'd forgotten about her diagnosis? Was his brain injury severe enough that he was that forgetful? Poor guy. And poor Princess if she wasn't getting her insulin.

As I said goodbye, I reached down and stroked Princess's back. No trauma. Surely, if she was getting her daily shots, there would be some anxiety there. Or maybe not. I didn't want to embarrass Oggie, but I'd have to talk to Hana about this. And soon.

After locking the door behind Oggie, I checked my phone and frowned. Still nothing from Will. I was dying to know how the interview with Mr. Kam went today and if they found anything at his restaurant.

As I was mopping the floor, there was a light knock on the glass. Goldie beat me to the door.

"I was just thinking about you," I said, letting Will in. The front of his dark hair was sticking up like he'd run his hand through it a million times in frustration. "You look really beat."

"Long day," he said, wrapping his arms around me. He kissed the top of my head and sighed. "Much better now though."

"Well, come on in here." I led him by the hand to the tea table. "I'm dying to know what happened with the search."

He fell into a chair and stroked Goldie's head as she rested it on his thigh. "Nothing. That's the problem. There was no sign of the TTX or any frozen puffer fish at Kam's. He could've gotten rid of it already, though. I interviewed him for four hours and he gave up zilch. Swears he had nothing to do with Russo's death."

I poured hot water over a diffuser and set the steaming mug in front of Will. "Do you believe him?"

He wrapped his hands around the mug. "I don't know what to believe at this point. I did get a writing sample from him. Also, we're trying to find out who this Dr. Trawets is. Postal Plus, where he set up the P.O. Box, has on record that he used an out-of-state ID, which turned out to be fake, and a local library card. But they either didn't bother to photocopy either one or lost them."

I cringed. "Ouch." After giving Will a minute to decompress, I let myself think out loud. "I even hate to say this, but besides Mr. Kam, Hana does seem to be the most likely suspect."

And Frankie told me poison is a woman's weapon of choice, but I'm not going to bring that up.

Will dipped the diffuser up and down in his mug. "We did rule her out because the pufferfish she served wasn't toxic. I just don't have anything other than motive, opportunity and that YouTube threat pointing to her. To bring her in again I'd need some new evidence. Like being able to tie her to the TTX ordered from VOC Bioscience."

I rested my chin on my fist, going over everything we knew so far. There had to be something to prove her innocence. "Hey, what about the note that came with the wine? Can't you get a handwriting sample from Hana, too, and see if it matches?"

Will's mouth twisted in thought. "I'd have to get a warrant to compel a long enough sample that it would hold up in court, and I don't have enough evidence for that. Although..." Will glanced out the window. "There is another way." He pulled out his phone and started a search. "I just need to find out when trash day is for her address. If I can get a sample of her writing from her trash that matches close enough, I can get the warrant." He rubbed his forehead as he read. "Her neighborhood trash pickup is Wednesday morning, so she'll probably put it out late tomorrow night or early

Wednesday." Placing his phone on the table, he nodded to himself.

I eyed him skeptically over my tea mug. "You're gonna steal her trash?"

"Well, no, not me personally. I'll have patrol pick it up. And once it's on the curb, it's fair game, there's no reasonable expectation of privacy, so it's not stealing."

"I'll have to remember that if I ever commit a crime," I teased. "I'm really hoping Hana's innocent, though." I sighed. "I do need to talk to her soon. Remember when she told us Oggie's cat, Princess, had recently been diagnosed with diabetes?"

Will still looked distracted as he said, "Yeah."

"Well, Oggie came in a bit ago with Princess and mentioned she wasn't on a special diet, which doesn't make a lick of sense if she has diabetes. I'm afraid he doesn't remember her diagnosis because of, you know... his brain injury. I have to make sure Princess is getting her medication."

"That's really depressing," Will said, shaking his head slowly. "He's still so young."

Mallory walked out of the back and plucked a sleeping Petey from his gated area. "All done. I'm ready when you are. Oh, hey, Will. You guys want to grab a bite? I'm starving."

"I could eat," Will said.

"I'll run the dogs upstairs. Be right back," Mallory said.

After Mallory left, I took Will's hand in mine. "Remember when I told you that I'd have to travel to rescue my father soon?"

"Yes. With Zach's help." There was no anger, just a touch of sadness.

"I'd like you to be there. When we go." I saw the confusion surface. "We don't physically leave, it's dream-traveling. Dreams are one portal into the Otherworld. So, you could just be with me in the room. Would you want to do that?"

Will squeezed my hand and I felt a wave of his relief wash over me. "Absolutely. I always want to be there for you."

His words brought a flood of emotion crashing down on me. After all the heartache of having to hide my magick and Will being so skeptical, I wasn't prepared to trust acceptance. Had we really turned a corner? Was he really going to take me as I am, magick warts and all? It didn't seem possible.

And if we successfully rescued Father, would it be too much of a shock for Will? Witnessing our magick in action and meeting my father, the source of that magick, was going to be the ultimate test of our relationship.

I slipped out of the chair, suddenly scared and unsure. I wrapped my arms around his neck. Would this make or break us?

CHAPTER TWENTY

Tuesday morning, I let Mallory open the boutique while I drove over to Hana's place. I needed to catch her before she left for the restaurant.

The convertible top was down on my VW Beetle. Glancing in the rearview mirror, I could see Goldie in the backseat with her muzzle pointed up, eyes closed, enjoying the salty breeze and morning sunshine. I tilted my chin up and took a deep breath of fresh air as I turned into the Paradise Trailer Park. My shoulders fell away from my ears. Yeah, we could learn a lot about appreciating the little things from dogs.

I knocked, holding an invite to Fresco's Waterfront Bistro's charity event as an excuse to be there. Daisy's barking began on the other side of the door.

"Darwin," Hana said, surprised. She pulled the gray robe tighter around her, her hair still damp from a shower.

"Hey." I leaned over to pet Daisy as she and Goldie greeted each other with sniffs and tail wags. "Sorry if this is a bad time. I just wanted to give you this." I held up the invitation.

Instead of taking it, she waved me in. "Not a bad time. Come on in."

I followed her inside. Daisy and Goldie started a game of tug with a rubber pull-toy.

"Can I get you anything to drink? I just made fresh coffee."

"Sure, that'd be great." I took a seat at the kitchen table as she poured the coffee and carried two mugs over. "Thanks." I slid the invitation across the table to her. As she glanced over it, I explained, "My friend, Frankie Maslow, and I are opening a no-kill animal shelter, so Fresco's is donating 20% of all revenue during this time toward the shelter. It's going to be called the Peter Vanek Animal Shelter, after a friend of ours who passed away. Anyway, we'd love for you to come. It's pet-friendly event, so you can bring Daisy."

She read the invite. "Sure. I have Sunday off, so I'll be glad to stop by." She glanced over at Daisy, who was taking a water break. "Oggie got Daisy from Florida Dachshund Rescue, so I've been donating to them, but we're always up for supporting any rescue." Smiling, she picked up her mug. "Thanks for thinking of me."

"Oggie is welcome to come, too, of course."

"Great." Her smile faded. "We haven't had much time together lately, and when I do see him, he seems super stressed. We'll make it a date."

I squirmed uncomfortably in the chair. "Speaking of Oggie, I need to ask, is his memory affected by the CTE?"

Tears sprang to her eyes. Her hand flew up in frustration. "Everything is affected. His mood, his judgment, memory, concentration. I'm really worried about him, but he insists he's fine."

"I'm sorry," I offered. I hadn't realized it was that bad and what a toll it was taking on Hana. "I can't imagine what you both are going through."

She wiped roughly at her eyes and sniffed. "We're dealing with it the best we can. Why do you ask?"

I shifted uncomfortably in the chair. "When he came into the pet boutique to pick up Daisy's treats, he had Princess with him. He didn't seem to think she was on a special diet for her diabetes. Do you know if that's true?"

Hana thought about that. "I can't say I've paid attention to her diet, sorry."

"Okay, well, I was just concerned, because if he has memory issues, he might be forgetting to give Princess her insulin."

She blew out a breath. "Unfortunately, that's a possibility. I'll talk to him about it."

On the way back to the boutique, I took a detoured stop at Helping Paws Rescue. Talking about giving an animal treatment for diabetes made me think about Sandy, and I wanted to check in on her.

Rhonda led me to Sandy's cage. She didn't lift her head, but her fluffy tail began sweeping the floor. I bent down and stared into her sad, amber eyes. "Hey, girl."

She pushed herself up slowly and came over, head hanging low. I rubbed under her ears through the cage, wiping a stray tear on my shirt sleeve. No recent trauma, just grief. "I know." I sighed. "I keep promising you won't be here forever. But you don't understand time, do you?" She leaned hard against the cold fencing. "If only Mallory would stay, then I wouldn't be alone, and together we'd be able to take care of you."

She lifted her head, her tongue hanging from a sugared muzzle. Her gaze met mine, and I swear she was smiling. I laughed. "That's a good attitude. You keep that faith, it's contagious." I pressed a kiss on her nose through the fence. "See you later, alligator."

❈ ❈ ❈

It was Thursday and the big day had arrived. We'd finally convinced Grandma Winters I was ready to attempt the rescue. I had a feeling she gave in, not because she actually thought I was ready, but because she was afraid Iris would move Father again at any moment.

"Hey." I greeted Will nervously as he stepped out of the elevator.

"You're shaking," he said, rubbing my arms.

"I'll be fine. Just adrenaline." Though, that was a fib. I was scared out of my mind. This was such new territory. Not only going on a rescue mission and confronting a crazy mer-woman, but having Will here to witness it. I'd never felt so vulnerable in my life.

I led him into the living room, where Grandma Winters and my sisters were laying out the supplies.

"Hey, everyone." Will cleared his throat. "Just let me know where I'll be out of the way."

Grandma Winters glanced at me, a leather book cradled in her arm. "Actually, you can stay by Darwin's side."

Will took my hand. "No place I'd rather be."

As we got comfortable on the loveseat, the candles they'd placed around the room all whooshed to life and then settled down into mellow flames.

Will tensed beside me. "Mallory?"

I nodded and squeezed his hand, shooting Mallory a chastising look. She was ignoring me though, completely intent on what she was doing.

The elevator door slid open and Zach stepped out. He stopped in his tracks when he saw Will sitting beside me.

Will stood and held out his hand. I watched Zach shake it reluctantly as Will said, "Thank you for doing this... protecting Darwin."

Zach's eyes flicked to mine, and he dropped his chin slightly in acknowledgment.

I silently thanked him for not saying we were bound, or it was his duty, or some other comment that Will wouldn't take lightly.

When Will sat back down, I blew out the breath I'd been holding. I shook out my hands and rolled my shoulders, trying to relieve the tension contracting every muscle in my body.

Mallory patted the orange striped throw pillow on the sofa. "Zach, you're here."

He lowered himself down, his eyes still locked on me. "Are you sure you're ready?"

"I'm sure," I said, relieved my voice didn't waver or squeak.

His mouth ticked up in the corner. "See you on the other side then."

We both lay down and got comfy. Me, with my head in Will's lap and my feet on a pillow.

Mallory pulled the footstool closer to Zach. Grandma Winters had a theory that Mallory could feed him energy and make him stronger by connecting to the plasma in his blood. I just hoped they knew what they were doing.

Willow's long hair hung over me as she placed two crystals on either side of my head. "I've added energy to these, raised their vibration, so you may feel lightheaded for a minute," she said softly.

An intense heat at my temples gave way to a wave of warm energy rushing into my brain, juicing it up like a revving engine. It took me a minute to get used to the high-pitched buzzing.

I took a deep breath and centered myself. After one more silent moment shared with Will, I closed my eyes.

The pages of Grandma Winters's book crackled open, and she began to read in her native tongue. Her words soon morphed into a haunting song, her voice rising and echoing inside my head rather than my ears. Everything fell away.

I opened my eyes and found myself on a small island, surrounded by crystal clear water. It shimmered with a silvery light, the source of the light originating from somewhere beneath the surface. There was no breeze. No movement. Suddenly I knew I wasn't alone. I whirled around. Zach walked out of the low brush behind me.

He stood next to me and stared down into the water. "Welcome to the Otherworld. The cave is beneath this island. We'll need to swim north a bit to give us cover. Ready?"

I thought about Mallory's usual quip, *I was born ready*. And I guess I was. Born for this. I knew from previous dream travels that I'd be comfortable underwater here, able to breathe and speak. I wasn't sure about Zach, though. I suddenly realized the risk he was taking for me. "Before we do this... I want to say thank you. You didn't have to agree to help."

He glanced sharply at me. "You still think refusing you anything is an option for me?" He looked like he wanted to say more but clenched his jaw and pulled away. "Let's go."

I tagged behind as he waded into the water. Its silky caress was the same temperature as my skin. Down, down we swam easily. There was no noticeable resistance on my body as we followed the curve of the massive rock. A glittery, black bottom came into focus. Zach put his feet down first and pressed his back against the rock. I did the same a few inches in front of him.

Even though the black ground felt like fine sand, our touch didn't disturb it. The edge of the rock was right in front of me, and I knew peering around it would show me the entrance to the cave and the sea-wolf guarding it.

Was I really ready for this fight?

I closed my eyes and focused all my attention on connecting with the water around me. The connection was instant, which gave me a boost of confidence. My magick was definitely stronger here. I could also feel the power boost from Willow's crystals coursing through me.

Zach's whisper sounded in my ear, low and urgent. "I'm going first. I'll distract the sea-wolf while you slip inside. Good luck."

I turned my head to ask him how he planned on doing that. Then had to stifle a yelp as I found myself face to face with his black wolf-form, red eyes glowing inches from mine. I put a hand to my heart. "Good grief, don't do that!" I whispered.

His long jaws stretched into what looked like a wide grin. Then he leapt in front of me and peered around the corner. With one last glance back, he bounded forward on four powerful legs.

Deep growls reverberated through the water as the two large wolves circled each other. The sea-wolf's lips were pulled back in a snarl, its eyes glowing green. Tiny swirls disturbed the water around them.

I latched onto one of the swirls with my attention and fed it, testing my power in this strange world. It immediately grew into a large cone, spinning wildly like a tornado. I pushed it forward. It collided with the sea-wolf, knocking it about twenty feet from the cave entrance.

Zach's big head swung toward me. Then with a few loping strides, he pounced on the sea-wolf.

I quickly swam forward and slipped into the cave, my confidence soaring.

I can do this.

As I made my way through the passageway with swift strokes, I stuck to the widest tunnel, ignoring the smaller ones that branched off occasionally. I was following my gut, which is what Grandma Winters had instructed me to do. Apparently, Elementals operate mostly on instinct, hunches and gut feelings in this world. Will would never make it here.

The water was clear, but the walls were slick with some kind of pink and green lichen or algae. Around a particularly narrow curve, I caught a flicker of purple light up ahead.

Cautiously I floated forward. The tunnel opened up into a watery chamber large enough to hold a city block. I pressed myself against the entrance wall and took it in.

Giant, jewel-toned stalactites hung from the ceiling. The cavern floor was the same glittery black sand that covered the ground outside the cave, but luscious green plants grew from it in clusters. Also, thick vines with some kind of hanging pods climbed the cavern walls. There was a round stone structure off to the left that looked like it could be a house. And off to the right, in the middle of the purple light, stood my father.

He was wearing the black suit, just like in my previous dream-traveling. His short-cropped, white hair glowed in the violet light.

I rushed forward. "Father!"

His mouth curved into a small smile. "Hello, Darwin. I've been expecting you."

I swam closer, eyeing his enclosure. There didn't seem to be any physical structure around him. "How do I get you out of here?"

He held out his palm. "Don't come any closer."

But it was too late. A powerful electric current wrapped itself around me. The uncomfortable tingling sensation had the added effect of draining my energy. With trembling legs, I pushed off the cavern floor, struggling to back up. When I was about fifteen feet away from him, the tingling subsided but frustration was rising in its place. "How do I deactivate that light field?"

"This is your element... Darwin, behind you!"

Whipping around, I came face to face with a furious Iris. Her lips were pulled back, showing off rows of razor-like teeth. Her eyes blazed with rage. "Stupid half-breed girl. You think you can come to my world and take what is mine?" Her mouth stretched open, and she released a high-pitched scream.

I tried to cover my ears but a blow from her tail sent me tumbling head over heels. I cried out as my back smacked against the wall by the entrance.

"Connect with the water!" I heard Father yell, though his voice sounded far away.

There was a buzzing in my head, making it hard to think. My limbs were heavy as lead. My legs weren't obeying my command to get out of the way as she raced toward me with a murderous, crazed look.

I squeezed my eyes shut and tried to connect to the water. Her high-pitched scream was interfering with my concentration. Panic engulfed me. My chest contracted.

Was this it? Did I fail so quickly?

Will's face appeared, his bright blue eyes inches from mine. Time froze. Peace replaced the panic as flashes of our moments together exploded in my head. Him tucking my hair behind my ear. Him holding me while we danced. Him getting down on one knee when he gave me the promise ring. Him going against everything he believed in to believe in me. Echoes of his laughter became louder than Iris's scream.

Instead of connecting with the water, I was connecting with Will. With the bond we shared. His energy was with me, enfolding me, giving me strength.

My eyes popped opened as a hot fire ignited in my chest. I gasped.

Iris was so close I could see the tiny burst veins in the whites of her eyes.

"Stop!" I roared, throwing a hand up between us.

A flash of white light exploded from my heart, sending her tumbling backwards. My power expanded with the light. It was both freeing and intoxicating. Stretching my awareness forward like invisible fingers, I felt the edges of the violet light that imprisoned Father. As my awareness touched it, it dimmed.

"You got this, Darwin," Father yelled.

I increased my concentration. The light brightened for a millisecond then, with a loud *pop!* It vanished.

Iris let out a blood-curdling scream as she pushed herself off the cave floor and launched herself at me once again.

Shifting my attention, I sent a water funnel spinning toward her.

My father rushed forward. Grabbing my hand, he pulled me toward the mouth of the cave. "Let's go."

"Stop!" Iris cried. "You can't leave me. I won't let you."

I glanced back. Iris had freed herself from the funnel and was racing toward us.

We faced her, hand in hand.

There was no time for thinking. Letting my instincts control my movement, I mirrored Father as he threw up a fist. Our energy compressed the water molecules together to form a solid, invisible wall like glass in front of us.

Iris hit it full force and fell back. Her expression morphed into despair.

After following the tunnel back out, we emerged from the cave.

"Oh no!" I cried. "Zach!"

The sea-wolf was on top of Zach, his teeth sunk deep into Zach's shoulder.

Our eyes met.

With all my focus, I created a compact, powerful vortex and sent it hurdling into the sea-wolf. The impact came with a yelp as the sea-wolf tumbled backwards. Though, before Father pulled me around the cave wall, I saw Zach struggling to get up.

❖ ❖ ❖

I blinked, disorientated and glanced around the candlelit room. Will's worried face came into focus above mine. My head still rested in his lap. "Hi."

He opened his mouth, but no words came out. The shadows beneath his eyes were more pronounced in the candlelight. He looked like a man haunted. He lifted my hand and silently pressed his warm lips against my palm.

Grandma Winters kneeled beside me. Her bell sleeve brushed my bare arm as she placed a delicate hand on my heart. "How are you feeling?"

"Not sure yet," I said, still feeling out of sorts. Iris's scream was still ringing in my head, so I was having trouble adjusting to being back home. It felt like I had a foot in each world.

Willow leaned over me and removed the crystals from the pillow. She brushed the hair off my forehead. "You did it, Darwin."

Grandma Winters wore a tiny smile as she patted my hand. "My faith was not misplaced."

"Thanks, I think." Pushing myself into a seated position, I startled at the sight of Father standing in our living room, embracing Mallory. "Holy heaven on a stick. You're really here."

His eyes met mine, and a huge grin lit up his face. "Thanks to you." He gave Mallory one last squeeze and then crossed the room.

With Will's help, I stood up on shaky legs. Besides feeling physically drained, my back felt bruised from where I'd hit the cave wall. I let Father wrap his arms around me. He was a good six inches taller than me, with a lanky frame like mine. The solidness of him grounded me, and the feeling of being in a dream dissipated.

"You did good," he whispered, cupping my face with his long fingers. Candlelight flickered in his clear, green eyes. "I'm so proud of you."

"I have so many questions," I said, pushing the words past the lump in my throat. He hadn't been with us for almost twenty years. Where to even begin?

"I know. We have plenty of time now." Keeping one arm around me, he held out a hand to Will. "Detective Will Blake, I presume?"

Will shook it. "Yes, sir. Nice to finally meet you."

"Likewise." Father tilted his head, really studying Will, and then nodded to himself.

"Y'all, I hate to break up the happy reunion, but Zach isn't back yet," Mallory called. She was leaning over Zach, checking his pulse with two fingers on his neck. Her other hand was pressing a towel into Zach's shoulder. "Well, he's still alive at least."

I rushed to his side and stared down at his motionless form. "That bite on his shoulder. How bad is it?"

Mallory lifted the towel. Fluorescent liquid oozed from four deep puncture wounds. "Not life-threatening. He heals quickly. I've already watched a deep claw mark heal on his neck."

I bit my thumbnail. "So why isn't he back yet? Grandma Winters?"

She walked up behind me. "I don't know. He should be…"

Just then Zach sucked in a deep breath, and his eyes opened. They met mine, red sparks pulsing for a beat and then dissipating.

My hand moved to my chest, and I breathed a sigh of relief. "Thank heavens." If something had happened to him because of me, I'd never be able to forgive myself.

Grandma Winters stood stoically beside me. "Welcome back."

Father rested his hands on my shoulders and watched as Zach slowly sat up. "I guess a thank you is in order for you, too, Mr. Faraday." He held out a hand.

Zach accepted it, nodding once.

"Yes, thank you," Willow said to Zach, smiling at him for the first time ever. Then she clasped her hands together. "Well, of course y'all have to tell us about the rescue. We'll never be able to sleep now."

I pulled out the leftover banana bread while Grandma Winters made tea. Mallory let the animals out of the bedroom, took the dogs outside, and then we all settled back down in the living room. I snuggled up against Will's chest as Father, Zach and I took turns relaying the events of the rescue.

Then with Lucky curled up in his lap, Father told us stories about his life and his time with Iris. He asked about Mom and said he'd be leaving in the morning to go to her. I waited to see if my sisters mentioned going back with him, but they didn't.

I caught Zach watching me intently a few times and wondered what was going through his mind.

It was after one in the morning when Will finally left, looking a bit wide-eyed and worn-out. At least he smiled when we said goodbye and said, "See you tomorrow." It felt like a huge battle had been won, and not just against Iris.

Zach carried in a few empty teacups to deposit in the sink. The others had dragged their tired bones up to bed, so we ended up alone in the kitchen together.

Zach abruptly turned. "Can we talk?"

I crossed my arms, leaned against the counter and fortified myself against his charm. "Sure. What's on your mind?"

He rocked back and forth on the heels of his black boots and then ran a hand through his hair. "Look, I'm sure it's no secret how I feel about you. That I think we belong together." He held up his hand as I opened my mouth. "Please, just let me get this out."

I frowned but nodded for him to continue.

"The thing is… tonight I realized that in the end, love means supporting the person you love in getting what they want, what will make them happy. And if being with Will is what makes you happy, then…" his eyes squeezed shut for a moment. "Then I support that. I won't interfere."

I stood frozen, so many things pulling my mind in so many directions.

Did he just say he loved me? And in the next breath he's letting me go? He won't be in my life anymore? Is that what I want? I don't want to lose him as a friend, but… No, that's selfish, I have to let him go. It's for the best.

"Really?" The word sounded sad to my own ears.

His slight smile echoed my sadness as he held up two fingers in a V. "Jinn's honor."

I gripped the edge of the counter as a wave of his pain washed over me. "You're a good guy, Zach."

He scoffed. "Don't let that get out. I have a reputation to protect." Then his smile faded, and he took a step toward me. "And I am still bound to protect you. So, the detective better not hurt you."

I raised my chin to look him in the eye. "He's a good guy, too."

Zach held my gaze until the elevator door closed. A soft ache of disappointment squeezed my heart. I sure would miss having him around. He'd been the first person, outside of my family, who'd known about my magick and accepted me for who I was.

I flicked off the kitchen light. "Goldie, time for bed, girl." I watched her jump from the sofa and stretch. Tomorrow is another day. And the first time Father would be around to answer all our questions.

CHAPTER TWENTY-ONE

Friday morning, we all rose early and gathered around the table for blueberry pancakes and tea with Father. I studied him as he listened intently to Willow talk about the Tocobaga Indian Burial Mound here and how some folks believe the site inspired the story of Pocahontas.

I resembled him the most. Same long, lanky frame, same winter-white locks and alabaster skin. Mallory had his green eyes, though. Willow looked just like Mom, with her dark hair and chestnut eyes.

Willow's face was flush with pleasure as she explained, "The real story, however, is about a Spanish sailor, Juan Ortiz, being saved from certain death by the Chief's daughter."

"Like you, I always found human history fascinating." Father flashed Willow a genuine smile before taking a bite of pancake. "And these are delicious. Just like your mom used to make," he said around the mouthful.

It'd been twenty years since I'd last seen Father. But even before that, he hadn't lived with us, so I only had a handful of fuzzy memories of him. Mom had seemed to understand this arrangement but would never talk about it. And then he'd disappeared from our lives all together. Now I understood why.

He was nothing like I imagined him to be. I'd always thought of him as this unreachable man full of secrets. But he seemed genuine, warm and open.

With a start, I realized that this changed the way I viewed our magick. Because I'd never been sure of where it came from, of what its true source was, I could never be sure it came from a place of good. Now I knew, whatever our father was, he wasn't a bad man. The gifts he'd passed down to us weren't bad, either.

I shifted my focus to Mallory, who hadn't left his side all morning. I understood her fascination. He was the father she'd only known through stories.

She sat beside him in her band t-shirt, hair pulled up in a messy bun, a goofy smile plastered on her face, looking like a kid again. It'd been awhile since I'd seen her so relaxed and happy.

Goldie plopped her paw up on Father's lap, her eyes fixed on his face.

He stroked her head then turned to me. "She wants to know if you have any bacon."

My fork paused midway to my mouth, I stared at Goldie. She turned and stared back at me, ears pushed forward.

"Bacon?" I said with a laugh.

Goldie let out a sharp *woof!*

"No bacon. But..." Excitement straightened my back. "So, you can communicate with animals? Like know their thoughts?"

Father gave Goldie one last scratch before she scooted back under the table. "All living creatures, yes. I can hear their thoughts, feel their emotions, sense their perceptions. It's all energy signatures in the Universal Field. As the first born, you inherited this ability, also. You didn't know?"

I shook my head. "Not like that. I mean, if animals have had recent trauma, I can get a vision from that, but no. I can't just pick up a thought like they want bacon."

He threw a questioning glance at Grandma Winters.

She shrugged a slight shoulder. "I was respecting their mother's wishes. She wanted them to live as normal a life as possible. I was allowed to work with the elemental magick only and only for control so they could hide it."

Father nodded then turned back to me. "Well, that limitation could be just a consequence of the way your human brain is structured, or those gifts could expand as you use them. I'll be glad to help you if you'd like."

A laugh escaped me. "I'm not so sure I want to hear my dog asking for bacon fifty times a day."

Mallory pushed her empty plate away. "Yeah, but you could ask Lucky why she hates Zach so much."

I forced a smile then took a sip of tea to help swallow the sudden lump in my throat at the mention of his name.

The hour flew by. Before I knew it, it was time to get the pet boutique ready to open. Also, time for Father to head off to Savannah to surprise Mom. What I wouldn't give to see her face. She was going to be over the moon. An ache of sorrow squeezed my chest, restricting my breath. It had been a little over a year since Mom and I had talked, and I missed her like crazy.

When it was my turn to say goodbye, Father rested his hands on my shoulders and looked into my eyes. "I hope you know how special it is to find someone who doesn't run scared from who you are."

I frowned. "Are you talking about Zach or Will?"

He chuckled knowingly. "I guess I should've said a *human* who doesn't run scared from who you are." He winked. "Follow your heart. It'll never lead you astray."

"So, you don't regret falling in love with Mom and all the trouble it got you into?"

His eyes widened in surprise as he said, "Absolutely not. Your mom, and you girls, make my life worth living. I'd pay the price a thousand times over to have you."

Tears welled up in my eyes. I didn't realize how much I'd needed to hear him say that. "Speaking of Mom. She hasn't forgiven me for leaving her. Think you can put in a good word for me?"

He hugged me tight and then gently wiped my tear away with his thumb. "I'll talk to her, don't worry. I'll help her see that you needed your independence, to find your own path in this world. That you leaving wasn't personal."

"Thanks." I wanted to believe him, but I wasn't sure he could work that kind of magic.

After he'd gone, I kept waiting for my sisters to tell me they were joining him, but they hadn't said a word about it yet. Grandma Winters hadn't announced how much longer she'd be with us, either. Now that her job here was done, she'd probably go back to the Otherworld. It sure was nice having her around, though.

I was dragging all day from lack of sleep and was getting worried that I hadn't heard from Will yet. What if he'd changed his mind after seeing my father suddenly appear in our living room and decided it was all too much. *Could I blame him?* I tried hard to push those thoughts away and stay busy. But, by the time he showed up at closing time, I was so relieved I couldn't stop the tears from coming as I threw myself into his arms.

"Hey, what's going on?" He lifted my chin, distress flickering across his face. "Something happen?"

I stared into his eyes and decided to start being honest with him about my feelings. "I was just worried, since I hadn't heard from you all day. That maybe you'd got scared off with the whole thing last night."

The corners of his mouth ticked up in a smile. "Don't worry. I'm not going anywhere. In fact, tonight I have to stop by the hospital to see Mr. Rocheck. You want to come with me? We can grab dinner after."

The tension drained from my body. "Sure. Is Spider able to talk now?"

"I'm not sure. But an officer did find a note in Hana's trash to compare to the one delivered to Russo with the wine bottle. Our handwriting expert thinks it's a preliminary match. It's a small sample, but it had the word "you" in it like in the note. It's enough of a match to get a warrant to compel her to come in and give a longer sample. So,

I want to give Mr. Rocheck another chance to ID her. The doctor says he's more coherent now."

My shoulders fell and a pit formed in my stomach. "I really didn't think it was her. I was really hoping it wasn't."

-⁕- -⁕- -⁕-

I sat across from Will in the restaurant booth, watching him struggle to read the menu. His attention kept drifting to the activity on the sidewalk through the window. I knew he couldn't get his mind off the Russo case, and I was right there with him.

The hospital visit hadn't gone the way Will had hoped. Spider wasn't talking yet, but he was able to shake his head "no" when Will showed him the photo of Hana and asked if she'd been the one who'd paid him to deliver the wine.

I was secretly relieved, though I knew Will hadn't completely ruled her out because of the preliminary match on the handwriting sample. Also, because he couldn't be sure that Spider's overdose hadn't damaged his memory to the point where he just wouldn't be able to remember who'd paid him.

"May I suggest the Seafood Risotto?" I teased him.

"Sorry." He rubbed his eyes and pulled his attention back to the menu. Then, shutting it abruptly he added, "You know what? That sounds perfect."

I reached across the table and slipped my hand in his. "You'll figure it out. I have complete faith in you."

Will rested his other hand on top of mine. "That makes one of us. I just can't shake the feeling I'm missing something important."

We were both staring out the window, lost in thought, when the waiter came to fill our water glasses and take our order.

When he left, I asked, "What about the TTX that was sent to the P.O. Box? Any luck yet identifying the person who ordered it?"

Will blew out a deep breath. "Nope. VOC Bioscience faxed us a copy of the medical license the person used, but it was a forgery. Scary what you can buy on the internet these days." He pulled out his notebook and flipped to one of the pages.

From my upside-down vantage point, I couldn't read much, but I could make out the name *Dr. Drew Trawets*. Something tickled my mind. *Drew Trawets.* Something was trying to surface.

Did I recognize the name? Had I run across it at the pet boutique?

I wracked my brain but couldn't think of any customers by that name.

Will rubbed his forehead then closed the notebook with a sigh. "Sorry, I'm not being a very good date. Tell me what's going on in your world."

I rested my chin on my fist, pushing aside thoughts of the case. "Well, Father left this morning. Mom is going to have a coronary when she sees him. In a good way. I'm not sure when the rest of my family's leaving."

Will nodded. "You still holding out hope your sisters will stay in St. Pete?"

"Yeah, I guess I am. It's been great having them here. We were so close growing up. It feels good to have us all back together again, ya know? Plus, like I said, I'd feel more confident that I could handle a diabetic dog and adopt Sandy if they were here to help."

Will cocked his head. "Maybe she's already found a home."

"No such luck. I stopped by Helping Paws on Tuesday, and she was still there. You should see her sad little face, too. Leaving her there just breaks me open."

"I'm sorry," Will said. "Have you actually asked Mal and Willow if they'll stay?"

"I'm too chicken. Once they say no, that's it. No more daydreaming about how nice it would be."

CHAPTER TWENTY-TWO

Sunday afternoon, Frankie and I pulled two square tables together on the outside deck at Fresco's Waterfront Bistro, beneath the shade of the canvas awning. Eighties music played in the background, mingling with the cries of seagulls circling the sparkling blue waters of the Yacht Basin. It was still early, but we wanted to make sure everything was set for the fundraiser. I'd brought Goldie, and she'd stretched out beside a chair, nose in the air, enjoying the breeze. Frankie had parked Itty and Bitty beside the table with a battery-operated fan clipped to their stroller. A smattering of locals were seated at the bar, talking and laughing.

Trey LeBlanc was in the corner adjusting a microphone. His long, gray hair pulled back in a ponytail and his guitar resting against the chair behind him. He was a local musician, who played often at the Beach Drive restaurants. Mallory had even joined him a few times, playing a duet with her guitar.

I'd brought some small items from the boutique so we could do an hourly giveaway with the raffle tickets. Trey would probably be the one announcing the prizes in between his Jimmy Buffet songs, so I needed to go give him the list.

My sisters and Frankie's boyfriend, Jack, arrived and we ordered drinks as more people began to trickle in. Goldie belly-crawled out from beneath the table to greet Lady Elizabeth, Sarah Applebaum's Shih Tzu, as they approached.

Sarah was overdressed, as usual, with glittering baubles on her wrists and ears and her hair perfectly sprayed in place, in defiance of the Florida humidity. She had her arm linked with a distinguished, gray-haired gentleman's as she greeted our table with flushed cheeks. The two dogs sniffed each other. "Everyone, I'd like you to meet Dr. George Abano. He's a heart surgeon, just retired here from Milan."

We all introduced ourselves and welcomed him to St. Pete. I smiled to myself at the irony of Sarah meeting a heart surgeon after her ex-husband shattered hers. I'd gotten a vision of her ex with his mistress the first time I'd touched Lady Elizabeth at the pet boutique. Even though I hadn't ratted him out, their marriage didn't last long after that. It was nice to see her smiling again, and not just because she was one of our best customers.

"You gotta try their ceviche brunch, if you haven't. To die for," Frankie said, as they excused themselves to find a table. "And thanks for coming out to support our new shelter."

A little before one o'clock, I spotted Will crossing Bayshore Drive. He approached the outdoor entrance but got stuck in the crowd at the hostess station. It took him a few minutes to get through. "Wow, great turnout."

Goldie pushed herself up to greet him. My sisters were at the table to greet him, too, but

Frankie was off selling more raffle tickets with Jack.

"Ladies," he said, catching Goldie's paw as she thrust it excitedly toward his thigh. "And dogs," he chuckled.

I waited until Goldie got her ear scratches and then snuck in a quick kiss. "A waitress should be around soon. Saved you a seat." I patted the chair beside me and took a sip of my white wine. I was about to ask him how his morning went when Trey's song ended, and he announced it was time to give out another prize.

"All right ladies and gents, time to get out your raffle tickets." He shook the bag full of tickets and reached in. "The lucky winner of this drawing will receive a Kong octopus plushie."

It was such an eclectic crowd. There were plenty of folks in shorts and flip-flops but also lots of wealthy women sporting Chanel bags, Fendi sunglasses and Dolce and Gabbana dresses. I'd been schooled on designer clothes by Sylvia, who would quietly point them out on our customers with admiration and a touch of envy.

"Any sign of Hana yet?" Will asked, glancing around.

My stomach clenched at the mention of her name. "Not yet. Did you get that warrant for a longer writing sample?"

He patted his khaki shorts pocket. "Got it right here."

I leaned back in the plastic chair and crossed my arms over my stomach. "I feel bad inviting her now, knowing she's going to be ambushed."

Will rested a hand on my knee to comfort me. "If she didn't do anything wrong, then it's not an ambush."

Mallory rolled her eyes as she fed Petey an ice cube from her water glass. "Good grief, Darwin, only you could feel bad for a murder suspect."

I ignored her. But thought again about Frankie saying poison was a woman's weapon of choice. There were no other suspects who were women. *Am I just refusing to see the truth because I don't want Hana and Daisy to be separated?*

Willow suddenly popped up excitedly and waved toward the entrance. "Kimi and Jade are here. I'm gonna go say hi."

Jade Harjo and her daughter Kimi belong to the Spirit Tribe, a group of Native Americans trying to keep their ancestors' memories and beliefs alive. Willow's always been fascinated with Native American history, so she'd befriended the two women when she'd visited back in February. They let her help out with things like collecting artifacts to donate to the museum.

I watched her beam as they talked. Maybe Willow's friendship with them would give her a reason to stay in St. Pete.

Mallory kicked me under the table.

"Ouch." I glared at her. "What?"

She motioned to the entrance with her chin. "She's here."

I glanced up to see Hana and Oggie making their way through the crowd. Hana was wearing a red sundress with a white flower pattern, her long hair in a tight knot on top her head. Oggie was behind her in a white casual button-down shirt and dark sunglasses. He had Daisy tucked under his arm like a football.

Will and I shared a glance as we stood to greet them.

"So glad y'all could make it," I said, feeling fake and a bit queasy.

Oggie seemed extra intimidating today. I watched as he sat a squirming Daisy on the deck so she could greet Goldie. I hadn't even thought about how he was going to take the news that Will, once again, considered Hana a murder suspect. He wasn't real good at controlling his emotions. Oh well, I just had to have faith that Will could handle himself.

"Here, have my seat," Mallory said to Hana. "I'm taking Petey inside to cool off for a bit. It's hotter than blue blazes out here." She backed away from the table with Petey cradled in her arm, his tiny pink tongue and black eyes shining.

"Chicken," I mouthed when I caught her eye.

She smirked. "Y'all have fun."

"Hey, girl." I reached down and stroked Daisy's long, floppy ear. Goldie was sniffing her friend enthusiastically. I could tell she wanted to play but there wasn't enough room. I dug out two bones from my bag and, after getting the okay from Hana, gave one to each dog. They settled under the table together to chew.

The waitress came by and took our drink orders. Will ordered another Coke instead of a beer, which I figured meant he was expecting trouble and wanted to stay sharp. We should probably order some food soon, but neither of us was hungry.

Oggie was listening intently to Trey's rendition of *"Cheeseburger in Paradise,"* bobbing his head in rhythm with the song. He seemed relaxed. That was good. Hana was studying the menu, her mouth twisted to one side.

A gangly teenager in a Rays ball cap tentatively approached our table. His voice cracked as he asked, "Mr. Stewart? Can I bother you for an autograph?"

Oggie grinned and removed his sunglasses. "Sure, what's your name, son?" He accepted the napkin and pen.

The boy shuffled nervously on his feet. "Dorsey."

As Dorsey gushed about Oggie's football career stats, I watched Oggie sign his name.

A jolt of recognition hit me like a punch in the gut. I froze, not even daring to breathe as I raised my gaze from the paper to stare at Oggie. *Did it even make sense?* I couldn't think. My thoughts were stuck behind a big white wall of shock. The music and the drone of conversation suddenly sounded far away as my heartbeat pounded in my ears.

What did this mean?

CHAPTER TWENTY-THREE

I grabbed Will's arm beside me. Thankfully, touching Will broke the spell and the vice grip on my lungs released. I took in a breath.

Will leaned in closer, keeping his voice low. "What's wrong?"

With a shaking hand, I dug an old receipt and pen from my bag. Shielding the paper on my lap, I wrote "Stewart" then looked up to make sure Will was still watching. Now he just looked confused. I steadied my hand and spelled it backwards. "T-r-a-w-e-t-s."

Will's eyes flicked up to mine and widened. He reached over and balled up the receipt, giving me a nod of understanding.

I stuffed it back in my bag, my mind reeling.

Is this proof of Hana's guilt? Did she use her boyfriend's name to rent the P.O. Box? Or was he in on it? Oggie did say he'd do anything to make her happy, and he was at the seafood festival, too.

We watched Oggie shake the boy's hand. Beads of sweat had formed on his wide forehead, but his smile was genuine. "You take care now, Dorsey."

I snuck a glance at Will. He was sitting back, staring out at the rows of sailboats lined up along the dock, their masts swaying together hypnotically. Probably trying to figure out how to handle this. Also, hopefully, considering calling for back up. We'd had a glimpse of Oggie's temper at the restaurant, and I really wasn't comfortable with Will poking this particularly large bear.

Will apparently had no such qualms. He removed his sunglasses and set his phone on the table. I glanced at it and saw the little blue microphone app on screen. He was recording this.

"Have either of you ever rented a P.O. Box from Postal Plus on Park Street?"

Hana barely glanced up and shrugged. "Rent a P.O. Box? Nope." Her attention was back on the menu.

Well, that didn't seem like the reaction of a guilty person. I almost breathed a sigh of relief. Then Will turned his attention to Oggie, who was sitting very still. They locked gazes like two bucks locking horns.

Oh no.

A drop of sweat rolled down the side of Oggie's face. He licked his lips then finally shook his head slowly. "You know I have problems with my memory, but I don't recall doing that."

Hana shot him a distracted look. "Of course not. You could just use my address if you needed something mailed here." When he didn't answer or break eye contact with Will, she looked at him more intently. Then she turned to Will. "Why are you asking? Does this have something to do with Russo's murder?"

"Yes." Will pulled out the warrant and slid it across the table. "And so does this." He gave her a second to unfold the paper. "We found a note in your trash that was a preliminary match to the note sent to Ms. Russo along with a bottle of wine that tested positive for TTX. So, I'll need a longer writing sample from you."

Hana's eyebrows pressed down, her eyes flashing with confusion. "What note? So, it wasn't pufferfish that poisoned her? I don't understand. You went through my trash?" She looked over the paper in her hand.

My attention flicked back to Oggie as he dropped his head. His jaw muscle twitched like he was chewing on something. When he lifted his head, his gaze darted around the crowd.

Every muscle in my body tensed.

Is he planning something? Assessing how many witnesses there are?

Oggie sat up straighter, his gaze coming back to Will. His brown eyes were damp, and a wave of his fear washed over me. "You still think Hana was the one who poisoned Ruth Russo?"

"I'm just following the evidence," Will said, holding up his palms. "It's not personal."

"But I didn't poison her," Hana said, sounding more tired than defensive.

"Of course you didn't." Oggie lifted a big hand and squeezed her shoulder.

Will's voice softened, but his eyes were still glittering with an intense, focused look. "I'm sorry, Oggie. I really am. But we have motive, opportunity, and now physical evidence with the handwriting match. A St. Pete P.O. Box was used to order TTX, the pufferfish poison that killed Russo. We'll find out soon enough who rented it, but it's not looking good for Hana."

"But she didn't do it!" Oggie's voice boomed. The tables around us turned to stare.

Hana rested a small hand on his arm to calm him. "This is all a misunderstanding, obviously. What note from my trash are you talking about that seems to match the note sent with the poisoned wine?"

Will was quiet, weighing something in his mind. Then coming to a decision, he told her. "It said, 'Left two steaks in the fridge for you. See you tonight.'"

Hana's face went slack. She sat frozen, staring at Will but her attention was focused inward. Then she averted her eyes abruptly. Her chest began to rise and fall like she was panicking inside.

Oggie reached out and slipped his big hand over hers. "Hana, look at me."

She slid her hand out from beneath his and let it fall to her lap. A tear slid down her face as she shook her head slowly.

A light breeze brought the scent of stale beer and seafood. Clapping broke out around us as Trey announced another winning ticket. I took my cue from Will and stayed silent, just letting whatever was happening between them play out.

Finally, Oggie's shoulders slumped and he deflated like a balloon. He brought his watery dark brown eyes to meet Will's. "I wrote that note."

Will kept his voice calm, but his whole body tensed up beside me. He was on high alert, which put me on high alert. "Oggie, before you say anything else, I'm going to read you your rights and inform you this conversation is being recorded."

Hana grabbed Oggie's arm. "Don't. You don't have to." Her eyes were wide, her voice void of emotion.

Is she in shock?

Oggie looked lovingly at her. He stroked her cheek with the back of his hand. "Your happiness is all that matters to me. Remember that always." He gave her a soft kiss on the forehead and then turned to Will, steadying himself. "I didn't mean for Ms. Russo to die." He took a deep breath, like saying those words had released some weight off his chest. "It was such a small amount. I just thought it'd make her sick, so she'd have to bow out of the contest. Then maybe Hana would have a shot at winning."

"Oh, Oggie." Hana dropped her face into her hands and began to weep quietly.

Daisy's head popped up above the table as she stretched herself up, trying to get in Hana's lap.

Oggie's face twisted in distress. "I'm so sorry, baby."

Hana lifted Daisy and buried her face in the dog's dark fur.

Will leaned forward on the table. "Take me through exactly what you did."

Oggie stared at the salt and pepper shakers in the middle of the table. "I ordered the TTX online with some forged credentials I'd bought." When he finally met Will's gaze, he sounded resigned to his fate. "I got the idea from Hana serving pufferfish, but I didn't actually want the poison to be in the pufferfish, so she didn't get blamed. I'd heard about how Ruth Russo almost got outed because she kept ordering the same wine. That's where I got the idea to put the toxin in the wine. It was such a tiny glass vial. How could such a small amount kill someone?" He choked back a sob. "When I found out she'd actually died, I was sick. I did that. Took someone's life." He pressed his palms hard into his eye sockets and moaned. "I'm glad you found out. Glad it's over."

"So, the syringes I found in your car, that was to inject the poison through the wine cork wasn't it?" Hana asked without looking at Oggie.

Daisy had her head resting on Hana's shoulder, against her neck.

Oggie dropped his hands into his lap. "Yes."

Her voice rose as anger began to push through the shock. "I accused you of using again. You said they were for Princess. So, she doesn't even have diabetes?"

Oggie cringed like she'd physically struck him. "I'm sorry I lied to you."

She moaned and pressed her face against Daisy's ear.

Will took a sip of his Coke, then asked calmly, "So, how did you get the wine to Ms. Russo?"

Oggie sat with his eyes closed for a second. When he opened them, the light was completely gone, replaced by pain and sorrow. "I paid a homeless guy at the seafood festival to take the wine to her with the note. Figured he looked like he could use the money."

Will shifted in his seat. "Unfortunately, that man, Timothy Rocheck, was a heroin addict. He used the money to overdose and is in the hospital."

Oggie's face crumbled. "No." He swiped a hand over his mouth roughly.

My heart went out to him. As an addict, it must be devastating to know you're responsible for someone else's relapse.

A deep moan escaped his throat. "What have I done?" He began to rock in his chair. "What have I done?"

"Why, Oggie?" Hana cried. "Why'd you do it?"

He angled his body toward her. "I'm sorry, babe. I was just so angry at that woman. She'd already caused you so much pain, and I knew you really were counting on winning that Golden Lobster Award to solidify Happy Sushi's reputation. There was no way she was going to let you win. But you have to believe me. I didn't mean for her to die."

Hana moved Daisy down to her lap so she could look Oggie in the eye. "Did you even consider the fact that I was serving pufferfish? Forget getting blamed for poisoning her by the police. Do you think the public could ever forget that?" Tears were streaming down her face now. She reached for a napkin. "And did you even think about us? Our life together is over."

Flattening his lips, he nodded. His eyes were bloodshot, his face streaked with sweat and tears. "Hana, I love you and I hope one day you can forgive me. I'm truly sorry I ruined everything. I will never forgive myself." With that, he suddenly leapt up out of the chair with more grace and speed than his size should've allowed. Covering the short distance to the railing in a few strides, he launched himself over it. A heron flew off the railing with a croak of protest and flutter of white feathers. A loud splash and spray of water exploded onto the deck.

There were gasps. Trey stopped playing.

Hana's chair toppled over as she jumped up, clutching Daisy in her arms. "He can't swim!"

CHAPTER TWENTY-FOUR

Hana rushed to the railing with us hot on her heels. "Oggie!" She frantically searched the disturbed water.

Will slipped off his shoes and was scanning the water, too. "I don't see him. Anything over there?" he yelled from the other side of Hana.

I squinted hard, trying to spot any movement as the water settled back down. "Nothing!"

Now people were pressing up against the railing, searching with us. Precious seconds ticked by with no sign of him surfacing.

I was pretty sure he couldn't hold his breath this long.

Frankie, Willow and Mallory gathered around me. "What's going on?" Mallory asked breathlessly.

I shielded my eyes with my hand as something caught my eye. "Oggie just confessed to poisoning Ruth Russo then jumped into the water. He can't swim."

"Well, that's not good," Frankie gasped. "The water out there's gotta be deep enough for the yachts to come in."

"There!" Dorsey, the teenager who'd asked Oggie for his autograph, cried. His face was twisted with fear.

Following where the boy was pointing, I saw the disturbance in the water. About ninety feet out in the basin, there was some splashing then Oggie's head breached the surface. He disappeared just as quickly.

"Is he trying to off himself?" Frankie asked, her voice tight with anxiety.

"We won't let him do that." Will hopped over the railing and dove into the water with a splash. He surfaced and began to swim with long, powerful strokes in the direction Oggie had last appeared.

At least I could help Will with this.

Where are you, Oggie?

Seconds ticked by. I could hear my own pulse in my ears. The crowd was eerily silent.

There!

Oggie breached the surface once again near the same spot, then disappeared. I concentrated all my energy beneath him, creating pressure from the sandy floor bottom and forcing it upwards.

Like a giant cork, Oggie's body popped up out of the water. Relief was short-lived, though as I noticed he was floating face down. I quickly churned the water beneath him until he rolled over, then held him steady.

"Looks like he's at least trying to stay alive out there," Frankie said.

Willow squeezed my shoulder and whispered, "Good job."

Will reached Oggie shortly after that, threw an arm over his chest and began to pull him back toward the restaurant.

The crowd around us broke out in a cheer, clapping and yelling words of encouragement to

Will. I created a current to move them along quicker, but not so quickly that it would look unnatural.

We all watched with bated breath as Will swam him toward the empty loading dock on our right.

Come on, Will. You're almost there.

When he grabbed the edge of the dock with his free hand, I gave him a boost from beneath the surface, lifting the water a few inches so he was even with the dock.

He rolled a limp and water-logged Oggie onto the wooden planks. They both landed on their backs. Will lay there for a second, his chest heaving as he tried to recover his breath. Oggie's chest was noticeably still.

Turning, I caught a glimpse of Hana fighting her way back through the press of people.

"Call an ambulance," I said to Frankie. Passing the table, I motioned for Goldie to stay. Though she seemed content to watch all the chaos unfold from beneath the table anyway.

"Excuse me. Excuse me!" I struggled through the crowd and broke out onto the sidewalk just in time to see Hana fling open the metal dock gate. Daisy was still tucked under her arm.

"Oggie!" Her sandaled feet slapped the wooden dock as she ran to him.

Will had pushed himself up and was leaning over Oggie doing chest compressions, when Hana dropped to her knees beside him. She let Daisy jump from her arms. The little dog sniffed me anxiously as I kneeled beside them. I rested a hand on Daisy's back as I watched Will try to save Oggie's life.

"Come on," Will muttered under his breath as he continued the hard, even compressions below Oggie's ribcage. His shirt was plastered to his body and water was dripping from his hair, running into his eyes. He didn't seem to notice.

"Breathe, Oggie. Breathe," Hana half-whispered, half-growled. "I'll forgive you if you stay alive. I love you. Please breathe!"

Oggie's head twitched. Water spurted from his mouth. Deep, choking coughs broke the silence. Will quickly rolled him onto his side and held him there while he continued coughing and expelling the water from his lungs.

Hana grabbed her chest and collapsed back onto the dock in relief. "Thank you, Detective."

Daisy finally relaxed, sprawling out on her stomach, but she kept an eye on Hana.

When Oggie rolled onto his back, breathing normally, Hana crawled forward and rested her forehead on his sopping wet chest. Her hiccupping sobs mingled with the screeching cries of the gulls above us.

Oggie managed to lift a large hand and rest it gently on her head. His voice was raspy and weak as he asked, "Do you really forgive me?"

"Of course." She wrapped her arms around him as her sobs turned to sniffles.

Will and I locked eyes and he mouthed "thank you" as the wail of the ambulance reached us.

"You're welcome," I mouthed back.

It was so surreal that Will knew I'd just used my water magick to help him save Oggie, and he'd actually thanked me for it. I tilted my head back, took in the massive, white clouds filling the sky and let the gratitude sink deep into my soul.

I guess being a freak wasn't so bad after all.

CHAPTER TWENTY-FIVE

I'd brought Daisy back to the house with us while Will drove Hana to the hospital to meet Oggie's ambulance there.

Daisy, Goldie and Petey had played until they were all sacked out on the living room floor. It looked like a tornado had hit the place. There were squeaky toys, ropes and chews scattered everywhere.

I started gathering the toys up. "Mal, can't you train them to put all their toys back in the basket when they're done?"

She didn't look up from her computer. "No, but I can set all the toys on fire for you. That way you don't have to worry about picking them up."

"That's helpful." I threw a slobbery stuffed snake at her and missed.

Goldie lifted her head, considered retrieving it but deciding it wasn't worth the energy, flopped back down.

"I'm right there with ya, girl," I mumbled.

No one had felt like cooking, so we'd ordered pizza and were just getting ready to sit down when the elevator door slid opened. It startled me because we hadn't buzzed anyone up.

Mallory's face lit up. "Father!"

Well, that explained it. I had a feeling he was powerful enough to make the whole building disappear if he wanted to. But, watching Grandma Winters these past two weeks, I'd learned how careful they were with their magick in this world.

I was about to set a plate down when it slipped out of my hand, crashing onto the glass table with a clatter. A jolt of surprise zinged through me.

Mom!

She'd stepped out of the elevator behind Father. Dressed in a blue silk shirt and jeans, her rich, dark hair pulled back in a ponytail, she looked a decade younger than she was. But her hands were clasped in front of her self-consciously, and her eyes were cast down.

"Mom!" Mallory and Willow went to greet her. "What are you doing here?"

She gave them a warm embrace. "Well, I wasn't going to let your father out of my sight again." Then, holding their hands, her deep brown eyes found mine. "Plus, he made me realize it was high time to mend our family." She gave my sisters' hands a gentle pat and then made her way over to me.

I was hopeful, but still couldn't speak or move. I didn't want to spoil the moment, to have it disappear in a puff of smoke.

Her forehead wrinkled as she looked at me earnestly. "I'm sorry I got so angry when you left, Darwin. I was just... hurt. But I realize now that you're a grown woman who needs control over your own life. And I guess, well, I guess I didn't realize by trying to protect you from the world, I'd isolated you from it. It must've been so lonely for you." She reached for my hand and glanced back at my sisters. "For all of you. Your father also made me realize that I might've been holding on to you girls a bit too tightly. Not just because I feared how cruel the world would be to you, but," she closed her eyes, "because I didn't want to be alone." Then she wiped at a tear and smiled at me. "Wow, that was hard to admit."

The warmth and familiarity of her smile filled me with joy. "Oh, Mom." I fell forward into her arms. Her hair held the scent of the azaleas and roses from her garden. "Does this mean you're not mad at me anymore?"

"Sweetheart." She pulled back to look me in the eye. "I was never mad. Just hurt."

Father walked up behind her and rubbed her back. "But now we're all together."

"I can't believe you're here. I can't believe you're both here!" I cried as the reality hit me. Both our parents here. In Florida. Together. "Holy heavens! This calls for more than pizza."

"I agree," Grandma Winters said, carrying a tall, round strawberry cake from the kitchen, her eyes glowing cheerfully.

"Now how did you have time to make that?" Willow teased.

"Time is a human construct, my dear," she said, placing the cake in the middle of the table.

"That smells divine. And who do we have here?" Mom leaned over and scooped up Petey, who had apparently recovered from playtime and was begging for attention. He had on a blue t-shirt with "Diva" in white sequins on the back. "Aren't you just a precious little nugget?"

"This is Petey." Mallory said, fluffing the fringe above his eyes. "His previous owner was murdered."

"Mal!" I growled, shooting her a glare. Mom didn't need any reason to worry about us living here. Changing the subject quickly, I said, "Mallory's supposed to be finding Petey his forever home, but she's gotten a bit attached."

"Who can blame her," Mom gushed, holding Petey up to stare at his face. He let out a tiny *Yip!* And squirmed. She planted a kiss on his head and brought him back into her chest. "Oh, I think I'm in love."

"Looks like the feeling's mutual. And this is Goldie," I offered, stroking Goldie's ear as she pressed herself against my leg. "She's actually mine."

Mom leaned down and scratched her head, while still cradling Petey. "Your sisters told me you got a dog. What a pretty girl."

I glanced at my sisters, silently thanking them for not telling mom Goldie's owner was also murdered.

Mom spotted Daisy peering at her from under the table. "Oh, there's another one. Who's this?" She made some kissy noises. "Come here, baby, I won't bite."

I snuck a glance at Daisy. She was sprawled out on her belly, her head resting on a stuffed turtle she'd dragged under the table. She wasn't budging. "That's Daisy. I'm just dog-sitting while her owner, Hana's, at the hospital. Hana's fine," I added when I saw Mom's hand move to her chest. "It's her boyfriend. He almost drowned when he jumped in the bay..." I waved my hand when her eyes widened. "You know what, it's a story for another day. Let's just have pizza and cake now."

Will and Hana arrived while Father was telling us more about his world. "To be continued," he said, standing and shaking Will's hand. "Good to see you again." He glanced at Hana curiously.

I introduced her to my parents. Something I never thought in a million years I'd be doing here in St. Pete.

"I'll make us some tea." Willow cleared her throat. A ghost of a smile appeared. "I have some news for y'all, too."

After Will straightened up from petting Goldie, he gave me a proper hug. His body was warm and strong, and I just wanted to rest there forever. Though, a strange energy was pulsing through him, and it unsettled me. I leaned back and looked up at him. "Everything go okay at the hospital?"

He just stared at me for a long second and then caught himself. "Yeah, fine. They're keeping Oggie for a few days to treat him for pneumonia from the water in his lungs."

I eyed him suspiciously. He was definitely distracted by something and anxious. I don't think I'd ever felt this kind of anxiety from him before. And we'd been in some hair-raising situations together.

Something's happened he isn't telling me about. Is it Cynthia? Is she still calling him?

"Thanks again for taking care of Daisy," Hana said from her kneeling position on the floor. Daisy was stretched up, burying her nose in Hana's neck, tail whipping back and forth. At least *she* was happy. Hana looked like she could depress the devil.

"Anytime," I said, wishing there was something more I could do for her. Guess she'd just need time to sort out everything that had happened with Oggie. "Can I get you a piece of strawberry cake? Some tea?"

Hana pulled Daisy into her chest. "No thanks. I'm going to head home. It's been a long day." She stood up. Her hair had escaped its topknot and now hung limply over one frail shoulder. She turned to Will, hollow half-moon shadows beneath her eyes. "What's going to happen to Oggie now?"

Will was staring out the French doors, hands lightly resting on his hips.

What in the world has him so distracted?

I nudged him with my elbow. "Will, Hana wants to know what's going to happen to Oggie now."

"Sorry." He brought his attention back to the conversation. "Oggie. Yes. Well, he'll get to rest and recover for a few days in the hospital. When he's stable, he'll be transferred to the Pinellas County jail and then have his arraignment hearing the next day. There he'll find out what criminal charges he'll be facing."

"Will they charge him with murder?" Hana asked. "Even though he didn't mean to kill her?"

"Can't say for sure." Will shifted on his feet. "It'll be up to the DA to decide what to charge him with."

She adjusted Daisy in her arms. "Will they take his brain injury into consideration? If he was thinking clearly, he would've never done this."

"That's something he needs to tell his defense lawyer," Will said. "For what it's worth, I agree. His state of mind and decision-making process is clearly being affected by the post-concussion syndrome. A good defense lawyer will use that."

"All right. Thanks again for saving Oggie." She glanced at me. "Despite what he did, he's really not a bad guy."

"It's not our job to judge him." I stepped forward and stroked both Daisy's long, silky ears. She squinted her eyes in pleasure. "You and Daisy be sure to stop by for a visit at the pet boutique. Let us know how you're holding up." Hana gave a silent nod. I squeezed her shoulder. "We're here if you need anything." I planted a kiss on Daisy's forehead. "You take care of your momma." She licked my chin and I smiled. "See you both soon."

CHAPTER TWENTY-SIX

After Hana left, we all took our tea and conversation to the living room.

Petey was sprawled out on his back on Mom's lap while she stroked his pink belly.

"That's pathetic, Petey." I shook my head. Mom and I shared a grin. Her side was pressed up against Father. I had a feeling those two would be inseparable for a while. I meant Mom and Father but also...

I paused in front of them. "Hey Mom, I was serious about Petey needing a forever home. He obviously adores you. You should think about keeping him. Take him back to Savannah when you go."

She glanced up at me and then back down at Petey. "It has been awhile since we've had a dog." Her attention moved to Lucky, who was curled up behind Mallory on the chair. "He does good with cats?"

"I'm sure Sugar and Sage would be glad to have a new subject to push around," Willow offered. They were the ten-year-old cats I'd found abandoned in a box near the railroad tracks when they were just a few weeks old, and they ruled the house, including the other three cats, two cockatiels and a three-legged turtle.

Mom slid her hands underneath Petey and picked him up, pressing him against her chest like a baby. "What do you think, Ash?"

Father reached up and rubbed Petey's head. "I think if this little creature would bring happiness into your life, then we should keep him."

Mom's face lit up. "Then we will." She tilted her head back and whispered something to Father.

My insides melted like butter in the sunshine. "That's two problems solved today," I declared, taking a seat by Will. "What else do we have to do? Bring it on, Universe."

Grandma Winters pointed a finger at me, but her eyes were glittering with good humor. "Never ask for something you don't really want."

I snuggled closer to Will, knowing in her jest there was also a bit of warning.

"So, Willow," Mom said. "What's the big news you mentioned before?"

Willow set her mug down on the coffee table and clasped her hands together. "My friend, Jade Harjo, helped me get an interview at the Museum of Fine Arts for the position of Volunteer Coordinator." She beamed. "And I got the job."

There was stunned silence for a moment.

Finally, Grandma Winters patted Willow's knee. "Congratulations, Willow. I know working in the museum will make you very happy." She shot Mom a pointed look.

"Yes, honey," Mom said. "Congratulations. So, you'll be staying in St. Pete then?"

Willow's eyes found mine. "Yes." We shared a smile. Then she turned back to Mom. "I wasn't sure, honestly. But now that Father's back and you're not alone anymore, I think it's time."

Mom nodded and despite the tears welling up in her eyes, she smiled. "All I've ever wanted was for you girls to be happy."

"We know." Then Willow turned to me. "I won't be living here, though. Kimi needs a roommate, and I'd like to know what it feels like to really be out on my own."

"I understand," I said. I was just happy to have her close by.

We all glanced at Mallory for her reaction. She was sitting cross-legged in the chair, looking unusually pensive, with Lucky curled up in her lap. When she noticed the silence, she glanced up and focused on Mom. "So now that Father's back, you wouldn't be lonely if I stayed here, too?"

I held my breath, waiting for Mom's answer.

Now a tear did fall. She wiped it away with a brave smile. "I won't be lonely, no. But I will still miss you, so y'all better come home to visit a lot."

Mallory wiped at her own eyes and nodded. Then she smiled at me. "And I *will* be staying here."

"Of course." My whole body hummed with happiness. "It's perfect because, even though Mom's going to take Petey, I'll still have two dogs to take care of."

"I thought you only had two now?" Mom said, glancing around like a dog was hiding somewhere.

"Darwin's fallen in love with a dog at the shelter," Mallory offered with a smirk.

"Guilty as charged." I wiggled in my seat. "Mind opening the boutique in the morning so I can go pick her up?"

"Sure," Mallory said. "Guess I'm working for room and board now."

"You be sure to keep your studies your priority," Mom chimed in. "Above boys, too."

"I'm done with boys." Mallory unfolded her legs and tossed them over the side of the chair dramatically.

"Can I have that in writing?" I laughed.

Joy and gratitude had me feeling like I could fly. My sisters were staying in St. Pete, Father was back, Mom was talking to me again. I couldn't wait to get Sandy out of the cage she'd been living in, take her for walks, let her and Goldie play at the park. I bet she liked swimming. We'd go to the dog beach first thing. Then a bath for sure. Could life get any better?

I felt Will's energy amp up. There was that buzzing bee feeling again. *What in the world?* I glanced up. He and Grandma Winters were exchanging a look I couldn't decipher.

He was making me real nervous. I squeezed his knee to get his attention. "What's going on, Will?"

He stared at me for a moment, then pushed a wave of short hair behind my ear. "Darwin... wait, this isn't right."

My heart catapulted into my throat.

Isn't right? What's not right? Me and Will? Is he breaking up with me?

My mouth opened but only a croaking noise came out.

Will slid off the loveseat and knelt in front of me. Then he clasped my hands in his. "From the first day I met you, I knew there was something special about you. Getting to know you has been one of the biggest joys of my life. You're the kindest, most thoughtful, most amazing person I've ever met. You've opened up my world, my mind and my heart again. Given me back faith in people and in something greater than myself." He paused, tears glistening in his eyes, his throat tight with emotion. "I know it took me awhile to accept your special gifts, and I'm sorry for that. For being so close minded. But, I want you to know I accept them now. All of them. I accept all of you and love all of you. Which is why..." He let go of my hand and reached into his pocket. Suddenly he was holding Grandma Winter's pink diamond ring in front of me. "I was wondering if you'd marry me?"

My hand flew to my mouth. My eyes moved from the ring to Will's face, so open and sincere and hopeful. His face blurred as the tears came. "Of course." I flung my arms around his neck. "Of course, I'll marry you."

He stood up with me attached to his neck and twirled me around. We both were laughing and crying as I switched the promise ring to my other hand so he could slip the pink diamond onto my left ring finger.

My whole family suddenly surrounded us with cheering and congratulations.

As Grandma Winters stood there grinning at me like the cat that ate the canary, I held up my hand with her ring on it. "So that's what you and Will were discussing on the balcony?" She nodded. "Are you sure you want to part with this?"

Her small chin lifted defiantly. "Absolutely. We may not be related in the sense of blood, but we are family bound by love." She reached for my hand. "May it feed and strengthen the love you and Will have as you start your own family."

Defying our usual formal decorum with her, I sprang forward and hugged her tight. "Thank you."

"You're quite welcome," she said when she'd recovered from my enthusiasm.

Father shook Will's hand. "Thank you for accepting Darwin for who she is. That takes courage." He clasped Will's forearm. "Welcome to the family."

"Wait," I said, thinking of something. "Is this legal? I mean I thought magick and mortals aren't allowed to mix?"

"Don't worry." Father turned to me, his tone soft, reassuring. "You were born of this world, already half human. The Otherworld rules don't apply to you."

I blew out a breath. "Good. Because that's one rule I wouldn't follow." Then I realized something. Any resentment I had toward Father for being absent from our lives had suddenly evaporated in the light of understanding. He'd chosen love. And so would I. No matter what the cost.

Mom stepped over to me, Petey still cradled to her chest. She slipped her free arm around my shoulder. "I hope all your dreams come true, sweetheart."

I thought about all the things I had to be grateful for in my life. My family, my friends, Will, the boutique, our pets, the new shelter going up. Life was pretty darn near perfect. "You know what? I think I'm actually living my dream, Mom."

"That sounds like my cue." Mallory grabbed her guitar from where it rested against the side of the chair and started playing the first song she'd ever written and my favorite, "Love is But A Dream."

"May I have this dance?" Will whispered, his breath warm against my ear.

"You may." I rested my cheek against his chest and listened to the steady beat of his heart as his arms tightened around me. I was remembering our first dance. How I'd tried to stop myself from falling so hard for him. How I didn't think I'd ever be able to tell him the truth about my gifts and my family. *And now here we are.* My magick is no longer an obstacle between us. I'd call that a miracle.

I smiled against Will's chest as I watched Father twirl Mom and Petey around the living room. Willow was singing along with Mallory even though she couldn't carry a tune in a bucket.

Grandma Winters was tapping her foot, eyes closed, enjoying the moment.

I knew there'd be hard times again, that was just life, but I wanted to burn this perfect moment into my mind. This night where my family was happy and whole, and my heart was bursting with love.